D0720709

HUMOROUS IRISH TALES FOR CHILDREN

Published in 1998 by Mercier Press
PO Box 5 5 French Church Street Cork
Tel: (021) 275040; Fax: (021) 274969
e.mail: books@mercier.ie
16 Hume Street Dublin 2
Tel: (01) 661 5299; Fax: (01) 661 8583
e.mail: books@marino.ie

Trade enquiries to CMD Distribution
55A Spruce Avenue
Stillorgan Industrial Park
Blackrock County Dublin
Tel: (01) 294 2556; Fax: (01) 294 2564

© Eddie Lenihan 1998

ISBN 1 85635 238 2

10 9 8 7 6 5 4 3 2 1
A CIP record for this title is available
from the British Library

Cover design by Penhouse Design
Printed in Ireland by ColourBooks,
Baldoyle Industrial Estate, Dublin 13

Published in the US and Canada by
the Irish American Book Company,
6309 Monarch Park Place, Niwot,
Colorado, 80503
Tel: (303) 530-1352, (800) 452-7115
Fax: (303) 530-4488, (800) 401-9705

This book is sold subject to the
condition that it shall not, by way of
trade or otherwise, be lent, resold,
hired out or otherwise circulated
without the publisher's prior consent
in any form of binding or cover other
than that in which it is published and
without a similar condition including
this condition being imposed on the
subsequent purchaser.

No part of this publication may be
reproduced or transmitted in any
form or by any means, electronic or
mechanical, including photocopying,
recording or any information or
retrieval system, without the prior
permission of the publisher in writing.

HUMOROUS IRISH TALES FOR CHILDREN

EDDIE LENIHAN

MERCIER PRESS

CONTENTS

CONTENTS

THE DRUID OF FEAKLE'S TOOTHSHOP

In the days when Fionn Mac Cumhail and the Fianna were in their health, defending Ireland against all manner of enemies, human and otherwise, men so often got such a hammering in battles, especially with teeth knocked out by thundering blows from war-cudgels, that the women of Ireland could not but notice. And they began to behave accordingly: at feasts or other gatherings where many warriors would be assembled it gradually began to be obvious that a man with all or most of his teeth would be spoken to by women far more often than even a hero who had only a mouthful of stumps or gaps.

The proof of this was Diarmaid Ó Duibhne. As well as the ball seirce, his famous love-mark, he also had a beautiful even set of pearly grinders. Every time he smiled men had to turn away, partly dazzled, partly in shame at their own ugly gobs. But the women did the opposite; they crowded about him, elbowing each other to be near him, even the married ones. And the more he smiled at them, tried to excuse himself and shrugged helplessly at the men who stood envying him, the more attention he attracted.

Now, Fionn, Conán Maol and Goll, as well as most others of the Fianna, who had only few and scattered teeth, could at last ignore this matter no longer. One winter's night at a feast in the royal hall at Tara they were waiting, staring, drumming the table impatiently, as a flock of six servant-girls crushed round Diarmaid, all anxious to be of help to him while everyone else fretted impatiently for food, even King Cormac.

It was only when Goll, the surly one, let a bark and a curse out of him, that the feast was able to go on. 'Hi! Ye useless cailleachs, are ye going to stay there like oul' geese around a gander all night?'

That brought them to their senses, yes, but there was another reaction, too, and that from Diarmaid. 'Gander? Who's a gander, manure-mouth? If the smell off o' you keeps people away from you, don't blame me for it.'

Goll flung back his chair, fingers scrabbling for his dagger. Only that Fionn clamped his huge hand on Goll's, rose and barked 'Enough!', evil work might have been done that night, deeds of little nobility or honour.

Men went back to their feeding after that but the heart had gone out of it and soon afterwards the feast broke up in a sour, sombre mood.

Fionn, in particular, was not happy. This kind of thing could lead to worse. So he decided to talk it over with Taoscán Mac Liath, the royal druid and wisest of the wise men of Ireland. But as soon as he arrived at Taoscán's door next morning he found that his timing was wrong. The old man was in the thick of some spell or other and in no mood for small talk.

He cut Fionn off in the middle of explaining this new problem. 'Are you trying to say you're blaming Diarmaid because he's too good-looking? What kind of ráiméis is that? If the women love him, then more luck to him. I wish

I had his complaint. Now ... if you don't mind, I have a few things to do,' and he steered Fionn gently to the door.

'But surely there's more to it than good looks.'

'There is. Fine white teeth.'

And he closed the door slowly but firmly. Fionn stood a moment thinking, then sighed. What was he to do? A straightforward battle he could handle any day, even welcome, but these personal troubles ...

'Agh!' He spat as he turned for Tara.

At the gates he was met by Goll and Conán and they were angry. It showed in their every move, every word. Goll spoke for them both. 'Well? Did Taoscán tell you anything? Because if he didn't, I'll settle this – '

Fionn gestured him to silence. 'He said, "Teeth." Does that make any sense to you?'

They looked at him.

'Teeth? What are you talking about?'

'He said that Diarmaid's teeth – '

Fionn stopped suddenly. 'By the Lord Lugh, I have it!' and he hurried into the yard, past bored guards.

'Call Diarmaid at once!' he shouted. 'Tell him I want him in the Hall – now!'

Men hurried off to do as he had commanded but Goll and Conán were mystified. That much was obvious from the looks they threw each other as they observed these goings-on.

Fionn noticed their puzzlement and beckoned them to him, just as Diarmaid strode into sight, a young woman on each arm.

'Watch carefully an' listen,' Fionn growled, 'but do or say nothing.'

In a moment Diarmaid stood before them, his usual smiling self.

'I'm here, Fionn. Is there something that needs to be...'

He stopped, motioned the women away. Why were his friends staring at him so intently? 'Is there anything wrong, lads?'

He looked behind him, to make sure there was no one else they might be watching. But there was no one. Then, before he could say more, Fionn looked him straight in the eye and said, 'Smile, Diarmaid.'

'Uh?' Diarmaid's mouth opened all right but it was in puzzlement. Was Fionn having some kind of fit or had he been drinking the heather wine again?

'Smile, I tell you!'

Diarmaid tried to obey but his effort was a sickly affair, as forced smiles usually are.

'Wider!' Fionn commanded, and Diarmaid's lips spread in a hyena grin, watched intently all the time by Goll and Conán.

Other men were beginning to drift towards them now, wondering what was afoot, but Fionn scattered them with an impatient sweep of his hand.

'Hold it there now like that, Diarmaid, until we have a right good look,' and the poor man tried, as they peered, gestured and nodded to each other.

At last Fionn turned away. 'You can close up your trap now,' and he slouched off, followed closely by his two fellow gapers, leaving poor Diarmaid bewildered. Only when they were out of his sight as well as hearing did Fionn speak. 'Well, ye saw what I saw, didn't ye?'

They nodded.

'Taoscán was right. 'Tis Diarmaid's fine teeth are doing the harm. What woman in her right mind – especially a young, handsome one – would look once, never mind twice, at the likes of us?' and he fingered his gapped gums. The others did likewise, and for the first time in all their lives something so simple that they had never noticed it before became obvious: they were at least half-toothless.

Goll was first to recover. 'But wait, now. Wasn't our fathers an' grandfathers the same as ourselves, an' what difference did it make? Weren't they fine men! I remember when my father was laid out dead they had to stuff his trousers into his mouth to make his face look normal, an' did anyone pass any remark or think that was any way strange? They did not. An' my grandfather, he was – '

Fionn held up his hand. 'I'm sure all you're saying is the truth, Goll, but times are changed, I'm afraid, an' we'll have to do things different. If the women of Ireland lose respect for Irishmen, next thing they'll start is looking for husbands out in the big world, an' only Lugh knows where might that lead to.'

'But what can we do,' Conán shrugged, 'unless to knock out Diarmaid's teeth?' and he grinned brightly at that thought.

There was silence a moment while Fionn considered this. He also smiled. 'No,' he replied. 'That wouldn't solve our problem. It'd only make us look stupid, might even mark us out as cowards, that we couldn't face a man whose only fault is to have good teeth. I know for sure that it'd turn the women against us, an' we have more than enough enemies as it is.'

They could not deny the truth of what he was saying.

'But what'll we do, so?' snapped Goll. 'If we go on like we're doing we'll have plenty more nights like last night, an' d'you think Cormac'll put up with that for long?'

'Look, let me think it over,' said Fionn. 'If I can do anything about it, I will. I want to see this thing settled as much as anyone else. The last thing I need is fighting an' wrangling in the Fianna. An' I won't have it!' This last was said with determination.

Sunk in the business of Tara over the next few days – especially preparations for visits by the Emperor of Persia and both kings of Iceland – Fionn had little enough time to think any more about the matter, though he never quite forgot it. On a brief visit home to the Hill of Allen that week he mentioned it to his wife, Maighnis, and if she said little at the time she did not forget either. In fact she was delighted. Here at last was an opportunity she had been hoping would come her way. For unknown to Fionn she had been discussing this very matter of Irishmen's vile teeth with the local women during Fionn's long absences at Tara. And the conclusion they had come to was that there must be an improvement, by whatever means it should come about.

'Them men, they're shameless. You could take 'em nowhere, at least not if you had any bit o' respect for yourself.'

Now Maighnis did what Fionn could not have done: within a single week she spread word to the five corners of Ireland that whoever could provide a solution to this mouth problem would be doing great service to both the women and men of the land, service which might even end in an invitation to Tara to be thanked personally by King Cormac himself.

Within a few days suggestions began to trickle in, some from friends and acquaintances, others from women who saw this as an opportunity of rising or being noticed in the world. It was, perhaps, for these reasons that the greater part of them came from little kingdoms and unimportant or scarcely-known tribes.

Many of the proposals were plain silly, such as the one from the country of O'Donnell that there should be a royal decree against smiling, or that from O'Reilly's realm that all laughing should be done only in the dark of night. There was even a fool from Sliabh Luachra who felt that all would be well if everyone wore masks, made of leather, no less!

Luckily there were others within the bounds of the possible, such as that piece of wisdom from Muscraí, that all people should carry a pin so that as soon as they felt a laugh or smile coming on they could jab themselves back to seriousness once more.

'That's still fairly stupid!' muttered Maighnis, 'but 'tis a small bit better than what them other eejits were saying.'

Yet only one of all of them – from the little tribe of Dál gCais – caught her attention as being maybe the solution to the problem, and she lost no time in getting word to Fionn.

He arrived home in double-quick time, in spite of all the pressing business at Tara.

'What's this I'm hearing?' he asked first thing in the door. 'Are we going to be ruled by women from now on?'

His wife brushed his question aside. 'Shh! Don't mind that oul' silly kind o' talk. What I have to tell you now might be the start of something that'll benefit everyone. So listen.'

He knew better than to argue. 'Go on,' he sighed. 'I'm one big ear.'

She told him of what she had done and of the replies she had got. Several times he threw his eyes to the ceiling but when at last she came to the one that had seemed to her special even he began to listen.

'. . . an' I always heard that the people – the women, especially – of Dál gCais had great sense. If they hadn't, they'd never have survived against all the big hairy savages o' neighbours on every side of 'em.'

'Dál gCais?' smiled Fionn. 'They're hardly there at all, that crowd. You could barely even call 'em a tribe. More of a big family with notions o' greatness. Believe me, they'll never come to anything. Too smart for their own good, they are. I don't see how they'd come up with any answer to our trouble.'

'No? Well, listen to this, so.' And he settled himself to hear.

'This woman who wrote to me – ' Fionn twitched. Women writing? What next? 'She tells me that in a small place called Fiacail on the other side of Loch Dearg there's a man who can do strange things with teeth.'

'Hm! Is he a druid, or what?'

'She didn't say, but can't you or one o' the Fianna find out.'

'I will. You can be very sure o' that.'

And as he rose he felt that he should thank her but

since Irish men had, down all the generations from the beginning of the world, done no such thing as thank any woman for information they themselves should have possessed, he felt it wrong to spoil this fine tradition now. So he merely grunted as he shuffled off about the business of the day.

He stopped at the door. 'If I have to go there myself to call to this fellow, will you be able to mind this place without me?'

She gaped, no less. Her lips moved but no sound came for a moment. At last she snorted.

'What d'you think I'm doing here all the time you're acting the man up there at Tara? Counting the flowers? Singing to the hens an' the cat?'

He did not reply. No point in starting an argument, now that there was hope of good news on the teeth front.

Back at Tara he made straight for the throne-room but found Cormac surrounded by dark-skinned as well as fair-haired foreigners.

'The place is like a madhouse,' scowled Conán. 'We're nearly gone astray in the head from all the gibberish they're talking.'

And it was true. There were at least ten languages being spoken all together, yet the miracle was that Cormac seemed to be on top of the whole proceedings. He appeared to be making good sense of all they were saying to him, and keeping them happy in the process, nodding and smiling at everyone. Fionn could not help but admire His Highness in situations like this.

'He can be as thick as the wall sometimes but he has the royal touch, all right, when 'tis called for,' and he smiled with a kind of pride that this man, no matter how silly he might be at times, was at least theirs.

It was only with great effort that he at last got a message to Cormac that he needed a few words with him, and little more than a few words it turned out to be, what with jostling and shoving, everyone vying for a place near His Highness.

'I have to go to Dál gCais quick, Your Majesty. There's something there I heard about that could be the making of us when we have smiling or laughing to do. So if you wouldn't mind, I'll take a few of the men an' we'll be back before you know we're gone.'

Better not to explain in too much detail, just in case of accidents.

Cormac blinked. 'I haven't the faintest clue what you're on about, Fionn, but don't delay. Things are bound to get rowdy here when this crowd gets drunk, an' I'll need many strong hands to put manners on 'em.'

And as Fionn nodded and turned to go, Cormac added urgently, 'When you're passing Lough Dearg don't forget to bring back a few fine salmon, just to prove to this gang that we have fish better even than those of Iceland, because I'm sick to my eyes of their oul' boasting that there's none the like o' theirs.'

Fionn nodded, glad of a firm excuse to go, and knowing too that in two days' time, when they got back, there would be little enough food left, so anything they might bring back would be more than welcome. The chief steward, Murchadha Maor, said as much to them at the main gate. 'Fionn, two more meals like tonight's an' we'll be cooking the plaster off the walls. I'm depending on you. Don't come back empty-handed. I need at least a hundred wild boars, two hundred geese, five hundred rabbits, a thousand – '

Fionn clapped a hand over his mouth. 'Listen, Murchadha. If we can coax a dozen salmon out o' Lough Dearg there'll be nothing more needed. One thimble-full o' heather wine an' a slice o' that salmon, an' they'll be eating their own fingers. An' that's the time Cormac'll be able to make 'em do anything he wants. D'you remember the crowd from Macedonia that came here two yeas ago?'

He sniggered, and so did all the others at the memory of that visit. They had been insolent, those warlike men from the Eastern World, had demanded tribute, hostages and drink – no one knew why. They could have been arrested, even killed, but instead they had been welcomed in the usual Irish way – fed huge draughts of poitín, then praised and played to by reacaires and poets. Yet they had grown only more foul-mouthed, riotous and demanding as the night went on – until the heather wine and Lough Dearg salmon had been introduced. And in tiny amounts these had done what all else had failed to do: sent them floating, reciting poetry, begging to be allies of King Cormac in his next war with Lao-Tzu, Emperor of China, or anyone else for that matter. As long as he had more of that wonderful mix to offer he might even regard himself as a future king of Macedonia.

'He have two fine daughters, Your Highness' – they were already picking up the local accent – 'an' he'd be delighted – hic! – to have yourself in the family, he would.'

'tis a noble thought, an' ye say it well,' Cormac had nodded sagely. 'We'll consider it deeply, too, never fear.

As will your royal master, our beloved friend.'

And they had staggered to their ships, loaded with promises and some gifts, full of love for their new homeland, Ireland.

But now, here, on this early morning there was more to be done than thinking of the past. Fionn called for no volunteers, though he could see that many of the Fianna were ready to join himself, Goll and Conán.

'Stay here,' he said. 'Keep order an' make sure His Highness stays in good humour. Diarmaid, I'm leaving you in charge while I'm gone,' and with a nod and a salute he was off, his two companions following close behind, their hounds whining at not being taken along.

Many a time on that journey between Tara and Lough Dearg they spied deer, boars and other animals that they might have chased at another time. But not on this day. Business first. And even the wild creatures seemed to know they were in no danger for they stood puzzled near the pathway on their hind legs, watching these men who normally made their life so dangerous hurry past, their eyes fixed on the horizon.

Few words were spoken on that journey. There was too much on each man's mind that only journey's end could answer, questions like would they find their toothman? Could he help them? How would they explain themselves?

As it happened, things turned out quite differently than they had anticipated.

For one thing, Loch Dearg was in an ugly grey mood. Their first glimpse of it from the height of Cúl Bán, overlooking it on the north-east, was not promising. 'It has something on its mind,' Fionn mused, nodding towards Oileán Mór and the way white waves were break-ing on its shore.

'Maybe 'tis trying to tell us something,' offered Goll.

'That could be,' said Fionn. 'Look at how calm the day is an' how blue the sky. There's something not right, whatever it is.'

'We'll catch no salmon there today, that's one thing sure,' sighed Conán, and the others could only agree.

'In that case we might as well be doing our other business. We can come back here later on. Maybe things'll be calmer then.'

Easier said than done, for no sooner had they made their way round the southern end of the lake and begun the business of finding where the toothman worked than they discovered that he was easier looked for than found. One after another the country people they questioned denied that there was any such person in that region. Some even said that they had never heard of Feakle, or Fiacail, or whatever they called it.

'It must be a mistake you're making, noble person. Maybe 'tis at the other end of Ireland you'd find a place with a strange name the like o' that.'

And so it went on, until at last Fionn could hardly keep his twitching fingers under control. 'The next stupid gamall that lies to my very face an' expects me to believe him, I'll tear the head off o' him an' stuff it – '

'Easy now, Fionn,' soothed Goll. 'They're afraid o' something. Why don't we call a meeting at the next village an' find out once an' for all what's wrong?'

That was agreed to, and that was done, the place being a swampy turn in the pathway named Lúbán Díge. Fionn stood and shouted in his most commanding voice, 'Come out where I can see ye! I have questions to ask.'

From several of the thatched huts he could hear rustlings and whispers but no one appeared.

He tried again, this time in a hard voice, for he was losing his patience. 'If I don't see every person in this miserable place standing before me when I have my fingers counted ye'll be sleeping out under the stars tonight.'

It was a threat he had often used and it had never failed though none of those thus frightened had ever realised that Fionn could hardly count beyond five.

It did not fail now, either. First one old man tottered out of the nearest bothán, then cringed before Fionn. Then others began to show themselves, young and old, men, women and children, until there was a sizeable crowd huddled there.

Fionn was not impressed by their manner. 'In the name of Lugh, what kind o' people are ye, at all? Are ye Irish? Have ye any bit o' pride?'

No answer, only timid, hooded squintings.

The old man who stood nearest him and a little apart from the crowd, bowed. 'They're afraid, sir.'

'Afraid o' what?'

'That ye're the tax-gatherers o' the king, or maybe something worse,' and he flinched back as if expecting to be kicked.

'Us? Tax-gatherers?' Fionn laughed out loud at the very notion.

'D'you hear that, Goll? You're after being promoted in His Majesty's service whether you know it or not.'

He turned again to the miserable ones.

'We're no tax-gatherers. I'm Fionn Mac Cumhail an' these are my friends o' the Fianna, Goll an' Conán Mac Mórna.'

It was as if a heavy weight had been lifted. Within moments their hands were being shaken by everyone, and all at the same time too, it seemed. Where there had been only surly silence there was now an excited babble of voices and from that babble Fionn quickly extracted the information he needed: the way to Feakle and some facts about the toothman.

'Oh, he's there, right enough. The Fiaclóir is the only name we ever heard on him. Anyone'll tell you where to find him.'

'Hm,' muttered Fionn. 'If they're any way like ye we'll be a week looking for the place.' But he said nothing, only smiled and waved his thanks as they left Lúbán Díge behind – for ever, he hoped.

He was so relieved to be free of it and so anxious to tell his companions as much that he failed to notice the old man in urgent head-shaking conversation with one of the young men of the place or that young man dart away through the trees towards the west.

Nearly an hour later and several miles further on they paused at a crossroads to take stock.

'Will we go different directions, an' meet here again later on?' Goll asked.

'No,' Fionn replied. 'We'll stay together a while longer. We can't be far from that place.'

They were about to take the path straight on when a voice from behind made them jump.

'Well! Well! Searching for Feakle, is that it?'

Fionn's hand flashed to his dagger as he turned. But no weapon was needed, for the man standing there was tall, dignified-looking, and his hands were folded. They stared at him.

'How do you know where we're going?' Fionn asked.

The man nodded a little curtsy. 'We know many things in this part of Ireland,' he said quietly. He was not smiling.

Fionn studied him before saying more. Straight as a soldier. Greying hair. Watchful eyes. But quite at ease. Nothing to be afraid of – yet, Fionn decided. Better be civil.

'If you could guide us to that place I'd be very thankful to you,' he said shortly.

The other nodded and with a flick of his head beckoned them to follow.

If they had ever stopped to ask themselves carefully what they were expecting at Feakle, what the tall stranger led them to would still have found them unprepared. First they came to two little hills and passed through the valley between them. Then there was a stream, which they crossed by three stepping stones. Finally, maybe a hundred paces beyond this their tall guide stopped and held up his hand.

'Listen,' he said, 'and tell me what you hear.'

They did so, but there was nothing more than the babbling of the stream. Fionn shrugged, shook his head.

'Good,' smiled the tall one. 'Now I must do my job.'

'Job?' said Goll. 'What d'you mean?'

But it was to Fionn that their guide addressed himself.

'I was sent to bring you to my master. He is most anxious to meet you all.'

'One minute, now – ' Fionn protested but the other hardly noticed. From a little pouch on his belt he carefully took a piece of black cloth and shook it out. It was a hood of sorts.

'I fear I must ask you to wear this while I lead you to my master – and these for your friends,' pulling two more from the pouch.

Fionn took it, fingered the cloth. Not one bit did he like this idea of not being able to see. Too often he had witnessed evil tricks practised on unsuspecting people.

It was as though the tall man were reading his thoughts. 'Have no fears of treachery. You have my word of honour that no harm will befall you on your journey.'

Everything in Fionn's training and experience told him to say 'no,' but if they were to meet the toothman in the limited time they had it seemed there was little choice.

'Is there any other way?' he asked.

The other shook his head. 'None,' he said firmly.

So they allowed him to cover their heads.

'Hold my hand, then each other's. This will not take long.'

His voice was much dulled though the cloth was not heavy. And not a jot of light was visible as he led them on. Fionn – and the others, too – counted carefully the number of steps they took, as well as the lie of the ground that met their feet, soft, rising, falling or otherwise. All was not as dark to them as it would be to men whose senses had not been trained as sharply as theirs. Fionn was busily building up a mind-picture in case he should have to come this way again, when all of a sudden their guide halted.

'We are here,' he said sharply. 'Give me the hoods.'

They fumbled with the tyings, anxious to see where 'here' was, and as they blinked back into daylight he held out his hand. They passed over the pieces of cloth even as they glanced about them. And a look of amazement spread across their faces. For before them stood a huge, grey, stone building, larger even than Brú na Bóinne, with white stones set into it in the shape of a set of teeth. Fionn's eyes crept up along its massive facing and in spite of himself his mouth gaped.

The tall man smiled for the first time. 'You are suitably impressed, I see.'

Fionn's mouth snapped shut as he jerked back to attention. But he had nothing to say.

'There will be more to impress you soon. Come.'

And Fionn noted the little smile again on that impassive face. It gave him the feeling that something – something maybe not to their advantage – lay behind that grey and white façade.

But Conán now spoke up.

'The man who built that had no taste, whatever else he had. Sure if he's as good as we hear he wouldn't need to be advertising himself at all.'

Fionn agreed silently but the tall one froze, then turned slowly and stared hard at Conán. 'Tell my master that, if it pleases you. See if it will please him,' and he stalked away.

'I will,' shouted Conán. 'Every man should be told the truth, not lies an' flattery.'

'Easy, Conán,' Fionn cautioned. 'No sense in making enemies even before we know who they are. We'd better follow him. An' be careful.'

As they approached the door it was opened inward by unseen hands, a fact which made Fionn even more alert. And where was the master of the house? No welcome for his visitors? What sort of manners did this show? Their guide led them into a short hallway. At the right side, in what looked like a little closed-in sentry box, sat a man dressed in a white cloak, a heavy club by his side. Facing him was a door of dark oak. Fionn took in all this at a glance, as well as the whispered way the tall one spoke to the attendant, or guard, or whatever he was.

'Wait,' he told them then and was gone, leaving them under the surly stare of the man with the cudgel.

When he returned he seemed a changed character. For one thing, he was smiling, and far more eager to please, it seemed, for he beckoned them through the door and bowed as they passed in.

And there they stopped, amazed. They were on a balcony which stretched away to left and right of them in a large circle, doors opening off it at regular intervals. Below them was a sort of courtyard but not like that at Tara or any other fort, where one might expect to see horses, carts, guards and servants going about their various business amid all the usual noises.

Here there was business all right and people hurrying this way and that. But they were all dressed alike, in white cloaks, and, most peculiar of all, everything was going on in silence.

Fionn stroked his beard and stared, while his left hand fingered his dagger. Their guide broke into his thoughts.

'Come. Your presence is required now.'

He led them left to the third door and into a small whitewashed room.

'Sit,' and he beckoned to a lone stool by the wall, as he padded to an inside door and tapped gently.

'Enter!' boomed a deep voice, and he did so, with a low bow of respect.

'They are here, master, the ones you sent for. And none too clean, either.'

Fionn was so taken aback by this that he straightened up at once, fire in his eyes. 'What did that liúdramán say about us!? Is he saying we don't wash ourselves – ?'

He had no time to get angrier, for from the inner room now strode a man in garb that all of them recognised at once, the robes of a druid.

They rose respectfully, summing him up as they did so. He was short, dark-haired, with a little goat-like beard. His hands he held close in front of him, left folded over right, and Fionn noted at once at least two gold rings. He smiled and there it was again, the glitter of gold. But . . . from his mouth? Fionn looked closer. Yes, there was no mistake. His teeth were of gold, no less!

All three of them were so taken aback that they stood there foolishly as he threw talk and questions at them. 'At last! The men of the Fianna, eh? Fionn Mac Cumhail, as well as the bold Mac Mórna brothers. Well, well! Come all the way for new teeth, eh?'

They got no time to reply, even if they had wanted to, for he shepherded them into his inner room, dismissing their guide with a curt nod.

'Now,' he said when the door was closed, 'first things first.' And he began to pace the room. 'You came here to enquire about teeth, isn't that it?'

They glanced at each other, almost ashamed to admit it, but since he seemed to know their business anyway, Fionn decided it was better to admit it. 'We did,' he replied simply.

'Well, you came to the right place. Now, let me show you some things you may not have seen before,' and he led them by a back stairs down to the inner yard they had already viewed from above.

Now they saw the hurrying white-clad figures close-up, and every one of them – in jars, bags, boxes or in fistfuls – was carrying teeth of some type. And while they stood bemused a back gate was jerked open and a heavy cart rumbled in, dragged by four sweating horses.

'Whatever is in that, 'tis a fair weight,' Fionn observed, more to himself than as conversation.

Their host was suddenly all business. He waved the cart in impatiently, then quickly steered Fionn and the others in the opposite direction. Fionn was at once suspicious.

'Aha!' he thought. 'Something in that we're not supposed to see.'

If at all possible, he decided, he would keep his eye on the unloading of that cart. He did so, too, even as they were shown sights that would have kept a lesser man dazzled and astonished. For there were wooden cases here and there around and on the walls, some as big as dressers, each displaying sets of teeth on open shelves, teeth the like of which none of the Fianna had ever seen since boyhood. There they sat as if smiling out at the passers-by, big teeth and small, strong ones and dainty, some yellowish, others milk-white. But not a single black or rotten tooth among them. The more they saw the more unnatural it all seemed, for who could imagine a mouth without at least one gap! – except Diarmaid's, of course. The druid pointed here and there at the cabinets, then said proudly, 'For Rome and Greece. All of these. As many sets as I can provide them with. The sweet food that does the damage.'

Fionn, though interested, was only half-listening, for the cart had stopped now in front of a red door, and as they were led back towards the stairs he glanced in its direction. It was already surrounded, by grey-clad figures, but no one was attempting to unload it. Every one of them was pretending to be busy, swatting invisible flies off the horses, checking the harness and the like, but well Fionn knew they were all slyly watching himself and his companions. He could feel their eyes on him.

'Now I'm certain of it,' he decided. 'There's something in there that we're not supposed to be seeing.' Back they went into the druid's office, and this time they were invited to sit. The druid faced them.

'Show me your teeth,' he said, pleasantly enough.

They obliged, and he at once looked away, as if disgusted.

'Yegh! Easy to see why you came.' He drew closer. 'Open wider,' he commanded, and as they each did so he studied them, one after the other, a look of pain in his eyes.

'Very far gone,' he sighed, 'Very far.'

He sat then behind a heavy desk on which stood piles of vellum manuscripts, then looked at them in turn.

'Much work will need to be done if your mouths are to be put right.' He sat back, hands joined, fingers to his lips.

'Who will pay me for it?'

They looked at each other, shrugged.

''Tis a thing we didn't even think about, your honour,' Fionn replied lamely. 'But I'd say King Cormac might help out. In fact, I'm sure – '

'King . . . Cormac . . . is it?'

The way he hissed the words made Fionn stop, look again. The other's teeth were bared. The gold glittered again but this time there was something sinister in it, Fionn thought.

The smile disappeared and a faraway look came into the dark eyes. He nodded. 'Maybe he will. Such a kind man as your King Cormac, maybe he will.'

He rose suddenly, all business, it seemed.

'It will take time, what must be done. But I will see to it myself. Nothing less will do for the honour of Tara. You must stay overnight, and we have the very place for that.'

He rang a tiny handbell and at once their former guide entered – a little bit too quickly, Fionn thought – as if he had been listening outside.

'Take them to the nightroom. And no food. Drink, yes, if they require it but no food.'

The tall one bowed, beckoned them to follow.

'First thing in the morning we begin. Choose among you who shall be first,' were the final words the druid spoke before the door closed behind them.

The nightroom was a little dormitory, dim and bare, with one small window. Four plank-beds with straw

mattresses and one blanket each did not offer the prospect of much comfort but it was not of comfort that
Fionn was thinking.

As soon as they were alone he called the others close
to him.

'Keep quiet,' he whispered. 'Someone could be listening
to us.' Then he began in earnest.

'There's more to this place than I can account for. It
seems fine to the eye but ... I have a feeling ... that
there's something not right ... '

The other two looked at him but were silent.

'Listen,' he said. 'I want to have a look around tonight.
To see if I can find out more. What I want ye to do is snore
an' keep snoring as long as I'm out there. So they won't
be suspicious if they're listening,' and he nodded towards
the door. 'In the meantime get a bit o' rest. I have a feeling
we're going to need it.'

And so, as daylight faded outside they stretched
themselves, each thinking his own thoughts.

Fionn, though, was not idle. From what he had already
seen of this house he was calculating what he might be
able to do and how they could make a rapid escape if that
became necessary. But he still had settled nothing finally
by the time darkness gathered, for well he knew that in
cases like this one had to wait and let things develop.

After a decent interval of night had passed he rolled
gently from the bed and checked his dagger. He might
need it though he hoped not.

'Right,' he hissed. 'Ye know what to do. But not too
loud while I'm leaving the room or everyone in the
house'll hear.'

They sniggered as he crept to the door and tried it – only to find it locked!

'Blast it,' he muttered but beckoned them to start, so that he could do something about it. And after all, even if there should be someone outside, well, a man sometimes had to relieve himself in the night, hadn't he?

Gathering his strength into those mighty hands of his that had been the destruction of so many ships, armies, forts, he gripped the handle, then hunched his shoulders and pulled evenly towards him. For a moment there was nothing, except the up-and-down rough music of the snores behind him. Then slowly a splintering began, as plank began to part from heavy plank. Joints cracked as nails popped from where they had been firmly hammered generations before. Then the whole door collapsed in pieces and Fionn had fast work to prevent the boards clattering to the ground. The snoring stopped at once and Goll tittered.

'You're going to have a big job explaining that to the boss in the morning, Fionn,' he whispered.

'Yerra, tell him 'twas something you ate an' you were in a hurry to the small house outside. Couldn't it happen anyone!' added Conán.

Fionn peered up and down the corridor.

'Here, tidy up this – quietly – while I try to find out whatever I can,' and off he padded, left, into the gloom.

He met no one at first. Only when he came to the stairs did he hesitate for he could hear voices below, slow and bored.

'Sentries, all right,' he smiled. He had much experience in Tara of such men and their efforts to stay awake in the dead hours of the night.

What to do? Face them boldly? Or look for another way? He turned, crept back along the corridor, but after trying several doors that were locked he decided on direct action. He steadied himself, then started down the steps, whistling merrily, like a man with no cares, no fears of being stopped. The two guards were taken entirely by surprise when he suddenly joined them and were still struggling for words when he asked cheerily,

'Good night, men, an' where might a man make his flood? I didn't want to do it out the window, just in case of accidents!'

His approach worked. Far from preventing him passing they were all helpfulness as they pointed him towards a room further down the yard.

'Thank ye kindly, men.'

He said no more, only strode off. And he went to the relief-room, too, but only for a moment, because just then the main gate groaned open and yet another cart just like the first rumbled in. It was surrounded at once by busy attendants with torches and as Fionn emerged carefully and hid behind one of the pillars supporting the balcony he saw it escorted towards the same door as before, where it was received with the same flurry of silent excitement.

Unsure whether to return to bed or not, he was about to move when the two guards tramped towards him. For a moment he thought they were coming for him but they continued towards the gate, speaking lowly.

'Another fine load o' teeth by the look of it.'

'Yes. That'll keep him happy for a while more.'

Fionn saw his chance, glided back towards the stairs.

But just then he noticed something odd by the light of the wall-torches. The wheel-marks of the cart were clearly visible a pace away in the dust where it had passed close to the wall. But between them there was something else, a narrow dark stain. Fionn bent silently, fingered it.

'Blood,' he murmured and turned for the stairs. He was just about to climb when he heard a rasping sound. There, busy swishing from side to side with a heather broom, came a servant, blotting out the dark tell-tale trace.

Back in the bedroom Fionn had much to think of but little to say as his friends questioned him.

'Keep quiet,' he cautioned. 'Goll, you stay awake an' watch until daylight – an' try to think up a good excuse for what happened the door. I'll tell ye the rest as soon as I can.'

As he lay there over the remaining hours of darkness he wished he had the wise advice of Taoscán Mac Liath to guide him. But at least he had his oxter-bag. He patted it. If all else failed that was still there.

Shortly after dawn there was first rustling, then noise, finally silence in the corridor outside. Goll sprang to attention.

'Oh-oh! They see the door, I think.'

A scurrying of feet approaching, then Fionn and Conán heaved themselves out of bed.

'I'll do the talking,' Fionn whispered, and moments later he was explaining his midnight excursion to the leithreas to the master of the house, putting the best face he could on the matter.

Surprisingly, the other made no fuss, only murmured absently, 'It happens all right, sometimes. I'll tell the carpenter to fix it later. But now, to business. Have you decided? Who is to be first to have his teeth renewed?'

Fionn had clean forgotten about it, but he replied calmly, as if nothing else had been in his head all night.

'My friend here,' he cried decisively, pointing to Goll. 'He it is who has the good fortune – and courage – to go first.'

Goll blinked. His mouth gaped. He was just about to protest when a vicious glare from Fionn brought a sort of pause to his face, then a half-smile.

'Ahm ... yes. Yes! I'm the one, right enough. Never afraid to face nothing, me.' But he was not smiling as he was led out. The smile was on the druid's face and Fionn noted it, too. Carefully.

After his sudden election as first experiment Goll was still growling as he was led past several doors to one where two white-robed attendants waited.

'Can we watch an' see what's being done?' Fionn asked but they shook their heads.

'The master allows no spectators.'

It was said in a tone of reasonableness, so Fionn thought it best not to argue. He sat, as did Conán, on a bench on the corridor outside and waited his turn.

Inside the room there were shelves, more of them than Goll had ever seen in one place in his like. And there seemed to be teeth everywhere – in bowls, jars, bottles and bags. He stopped, confused, but the druid merely pointed him to a large chair in the centre of the floor.

'Sit,'

When Goll had done so, the druid asked:

'How many teeth have you?'

'Six, the last time I counted,' and Goll quickly checked again with his tongue. The druid sighed.

'Open your mouth till I see for myself.'

Goll did so, and as he squinted into that dark cavern it was easy to know that he was less than pleased.

'Not a lovely sight, eh! What does your wife think about all this?'

'Nothing. Her own are just the same.'

Little more was said, except

'Those six will have to be pulled out. Otherwise I cannot even start to work on you. Will you agree to that?'

'Will it hurt much?'

The druid reached behind him and produced an evil-looking pincers.

'Look at these, then guess for yourself.'

Goll licked his lips, hesitated.

'But don't worry,' the dentist smiled. He rose and fingered a small dark bottle from a shelf. 'Three drops of this and you won't feel a thing.'

He stared at Goll with those dark eyes of his. 'So, what do you wish?'

To seek to avoid pain was not honourable in a member of the Fianna, Goll knew. But he also remembered the great blow from Tuathal Cam Ó Flatharta's war-club that had smashed eight of his fangs at the Third Battle of Tuath Clae. That was pain that he would recall forever, a thing he would not willingly face again, even now. He pointed to the little bottle.

'Sensible man,' smiled the druid and measured the three drops into a tiny spoon.

'Open again.'

Goll did so, swallowed. And that was the last he knew about the doings of the dark man in white.

Out in the corridor the first hour passed quietly but two hours later when there was no sign of Goll his brother began to get restless.

'What's going on in there, at all, Fionn? Will I knock?'

'Leave it a while longer,' Fionn advised. 'Some things take time,' and he chortled as he thought of the state of Goll's – indeed of all of their teeth.

Time dragged on, and finally, almost at midday, the door opened. Goll staggered out supported by the two attendants, the lower part of his face hidden by a white cloth.

Conán sprang up. 'What's he after doing to you, Goll?! I'll make him pay – '

Fionn laid a strong hand on his arm. 'Stop, will you! Wait an' hear what the man inside has to say.'

And at that moment the toothman stepped into the corridor, rubbing his hands on a napkin. He smiled, that golden smile.

'That was no easy job but good work always takes time, eh?'

Fionn could not argue with that.

'Now, who is next?'

'You go on, Conán. I'll bring up the rear this time.'

Conán stared at them both in turn.

'Oh, you will? But how do I know that there isn't a plot here to get rid o' myself an' my brother?'

Fionn gaped, then sighed. Would the old bitter feud between his and their family never be fully buried and forgotten? Why did they have to keep opening these old wounds, especially at moments like this?

Better be firm, he decided. 'There's no plot, Conán. You have my word on that. If you're afraid, say so an' I'll go next.'

'Me? Afraid? Afraid o' what?' and he looked the druid up and down.

'Come, come!' that man now urged impatiently. 'Time is passing. We must begin now if this one is to be completed today.'

'Oh, I'll go,' snapped Fionn. 'Let him stand there an' talk to himself for the next few hours, if that's what he wants.'

This had the desired effect. Conán leaped to the door in front of him.

'No one is going to fill my place if I can fill it myself,' he almost yelled, and with that he·was led inside.

Fionn sat again, shaking his head at the silly way grown-up men sometimes behaved.

Several times during the long hours that followed Fionn attempted to visit Goll in the bedroom but each time he was asked by a door-attendant to leave it until morning, that Goll needed rest and quiet after his ordeal. At another time he might have argued but now, distracted as he was, expecting to be called himself at any moment, he did not insist.

But when Conán was assisted out of the druid's surgery and helped away it was well on in the evening and shadows were beginning to gather. Far too late now for himself to be attended to, Fionn knew, and the druid made that same very clear.

'No more can be done today,' he sighed, 'But in the morning we will continue.'

Fionn could see tiredness in his face. He nodded agreement and was turning to go when the other said softly,

'They must be by themselves. In quietness. Until all is complete. These two know what they must do. As will you tomorrow. These instructions must be obeyed if your visit is to be successful.'

He pointed to a third attendant. 'This man will show you where to sleep tonight.' He nodded, his door closed silently and Fionn followed the servant. He knew enough about the ways of druids not to bother questioning or disputing. They would do what they had already decided in any case.

At the door of his new bedroom the guide left him without a word, only a stiff little bow.

'This crowd are getting on my nerves,' and his fists tightened. But he pushed in the door, paused in the darkness, then pawed his way to the bed and sat heavily. A few minutes of stillness were enough to bring him to his full senses.

'What's wrong with me, sitting here like a fool?' he growled. And in the next few minutes he rehearsed in his head what must be done. First he must find out what was in that room that the carts delivered their loads to. After that ... well, he would wait and see how things developed.

As soon as he judged everything to be dark and quiet enough, he tried the door. It opened.

'Good,' he thought. 'They mightn't believe me if the second door had to be wrecked in one day.'

This time he knew exactly where he was going and how to get there. For one thing he decided not to use the stairs. Better to avoid the guards entirely. He could jump down into the yard from the balcony at a point nearer that door that was his destination.

As he closed his bedroom door softly behind him he noticed something else: a strong breeze had risen and rain was beginning to spatter the walls.

He smiled to note that several torches around the yard had been blown out.

'All the better for my work,' he nodded as he checked his dagger and padded on along the balcony. He was almost above the door when he stopped, crouched behind one of the pillars and thought a moment. Opposite him he could see the main gate clearly, and two of the guards chatting, wrapped in their cloaks. If he swung down, no matter how fast he did it, might they not see him? What then? How to explain that?

He glanced about. More pillars. More doors at regular intervals. The wind snapping. Little wisps of dust fleeing here and there below. Better to try a few doors first – and hope for the best.

As he fingered the latch on the nearest one he whispered, 'Taoscán, I hope you're awake an' thinking o' me.'

A draught of clammy air blew out against him as he pushed in the door – and a peculiar smell. He hesitated, but only a moment, then slipped in, and paused as the door clicked shut. He sniffed. There was that smell again, only much stronger. Voices, too. Many voices, talking lowly, at a distance.

'What *is* that?' – and then it came to him. The clammy smell of things dead! The smell from the pile of boars and deer after a day's hunt.

'But here?'

He had to get closer, to see this for himself.

He was standing at the top of a spiral stone stairway and it was from below him the noise was coming. He drew his dagger and edged forward and down, careful of each step, since it was almost pitch-dark. Down and down. Step by step. And all the while the voices grew louder, more clear. There were other sounds, too, hammerings light and heavy, and ... and ... sawing.

'Whatever they're at, they're busy,' he muttered. Then he stopped. There, before him, one step up and to the right was a door, a line of light shining under it.

He stared, trying to decide.

'Maybe it'd be safer to look at 'em from here than from below.'

So saying, he fingered the door, opened it gently and peeped in. What he saw, as much as he could see of it, stopped his breath. There below was a large hall with long tables in three rows from end to end. Each table was surrounded by those white-cloaked ones who had peered at Fionn so suspiciously the previous night – he could not forget those – and at the top of the hall stood three men who seemed to be supervising the work.

But 'work'? Fionn shuddered as he looked closer, then opened the door wider. An arm's-length before him was a little balcony where no more than two people might stand together. He dropped to his knees, then crouched forward and peered down between the wooden uprights at the business in hand.

It was gruesome. Like a slaughterhouse. Beneath him, at the yard-door, was a heap of heads, all bloody, and one man was flinging them up on to the tables with a pointed metal rod. He whistled as he worked, not seeming to care whether he spiked their eyes, mouths or scalp. At the tables it was worse. Those standing there were busily at work with knives, cleavers, hammers and pincers, some separating jawbones from heads, others chiselling out the teeth. Occasionally bones had to be hacked or sawed to get to the roots, but it seemed not to worry these workers in the least.

They joked among themselves, one sometimes flinging a remnant of a skull or a brain playfully at another worker further down the table. But the only time the three men at the head of the room intervened was when it seemed that any teeth might be damaged or lost. 'Enough o' the antics, Maolruan! Stop that, Murcha, or your own head'll be on that table tomorrow night.'

Every so often, when a pile of teeth had built up, a worker with a long-handled scoop would pull them to the table's end and into a large sack. They were then carried out by two others, blood dripping behind them.

Fionn was so disgusted he almost vomited. But he was fascinated, too, for he had never witnessed anything like this. Terrible wounds, blood, all kinds of maimings he had seen in plenty in many battles but this was new. It was ... dishonourable. No one's head should be treated like this. Even the worst of criminals deserved something better. And some of these heads, even with their bloody matted hair, pale staring eyes and open mouths, were still noble to the eye.

Then another thought struck him: where had they all come from? But he had seen enough, enough to last him a lifetime. Slowly, cautiously, he withdrew, accompanied by the sound of laughter and splitting of bone and the hollow clack as what remained of each head was flung onto a gory heap in the far left-hand corner.

'If the gods leave this house standing for long more . . . I promise I won't,' he snarled as he hurried back to where Goll and Conán were sleeping. And luckily no man met him on the way. For it would have cost him his life.

He sat on the edge of his bed for only a very few moments. He had already made up his mind. He would never accept new teeth in this place, now that he knew where they came from, not even if every woman in Ireland were to offer him her love.

'I won't stay here another minute. Or Conán or Goll either.'

In moments he was with them, shaking them urgently. 'Come on! Out of it. We're going. Now!'

They stumbled to their feet, only half-aware of what was happening.

'Here. Get dressed!' he snarled and flung their clothes at them.

Rapidly waking now, they scrabbled in the darkness, still confused.

'Fionn, what's the – ?'

'Never mind that. Just follow me.'

They did that, but awkwardly.

In the yard the wind had increased and the only torches still lighting were those at the main gate. Fionn was relieved.

'Now we'll be able to go over any part of the wall that suits us without anyone the wiser,' he nodded but the steely look in his eye spoke something else, too – that he would have smashed through the main gate itself if that was what was necessary to leave this vile house.

Within minutes they were up, over and out, the guards, too busy with their own discomfort, none the wiser. Which direction they were going did not matter at first. All Fionn wanted was to put much distance between themselves and Fiacail before daylight. And this they did, gradually correcting themselves by glimpses of the stars. It was still semi-dark when they came to Loch Dearg.

'Now what'll we do?' rattled Goll. 'We can't swim that.'

It seemed a sensible enough observation. But Fionn was in no mood for delay.

'Talk for yourself,' he replied and splashed into the water. 'There's no time for going round it. Come on.'

He saw them hesitate. He could have ordered them to follow but he knew well that mockery would work far better.

'But if 'tis afraid ye are, get up here on my shoulders an' I'll bring ye across safe.'

That did it. Muttering and growling they plunged after him. He could hear their teeth chatter and he smiled.

'Now we'll find out how good a job that fellow did on those fangs,' he gurgled as his first powerful strokes drew him away from land.

The further out into deep water they swam the colder it got but Fionn showed nothing, only kept up a streel of jokes and encouragement to the others. Suddenly he noticed something odd and stopped swimming.

'Shh!' he ordered. 'Tread water an' listen.'

They did, and were amazed to hear a splashing and

gurgling all around them.

'What in the name of Lugh is that?' panted Conán.

Fionn did not answer at once. He was trying to make some sense of it himself. Then it hit him! Fish; salmon, pike and others. And they were laughing at them, mocking them and breaking wind in their direction. Fionn had heard Taoscán speak of such a thing once but had dismissed it as a joke. But it was no joke. He was disgusted at this lack of manners and courtesy by the fish of Dál gCais.

'Boyne fish wouldn't do the like o' that,' he snorted, 'but if they keep on at it I'll teach 'em a lesson they won't forget.'

Just then he felt something brush along his left leg and knew it was a pike slyly getting ready to have a meal at his expense. It was time to act.

Leaving the other two puffing and goggle-eyed he spun upside down in the water, probed like lightning down into the dark and sank his fingers into cold clammy flesh. He heaved his prey clear of the surface and there, writhing, was a pike almost twice as big as himself.

'Haha, me lad,' he chuckled as he treaded water furiously. 'Trying to take a low advantage o' me an' I in a hurry, eh? Well, I'll put manners on you right now, so I will.'

He said no more, only swung the pike over and behind his head while his legs beat the water to foam like mill-wheels. Then with a 'splat' he brought the cold body head-first down on Conán's bald head, all he could identify that was solid in the gloom.

That first shocking crack of heads left both Conán and

the fish dazed but at the second blow at least the man reacted. He let out a screech which became a howl, then a croaking splutter as blow followed on blow.

Goll tried to intervene now, but Fionn had his battle-madness on him or what looked very like it.

'Stop, you lunatic! Are you trying to kill my brother?'

His hands scrabbled for Fionn's shoulders and he began to wrestle him to a sort of calmness, all the time bellowing 'Will you calm down! None of us'll see Tara again if you don't quieten yourself.'

By now the people of both sides of the lake were flocking to the shore in all stages of dress and undress. They had been jolted out of their dreams by the horrid yelling, and word was spreading like the wind of sinister human sacrifice in progress out there in the dark, or some furious battle among the Tuatha Dé Danann.

Imagine the surprise – and relief – of those on the Tipperary side at least when they saw no worse than three bedraggled warriors staggering ashore at Gort Mór, one of them dragging one of the biggest fish they had ever seen. No words were spoken. The natives knew well enough that to question now would be a dangerous mistake. The crowd parted as Fionn, his flapping burden thrown over his shoulders, trudged up the shore and stalked grimly eastwards, Goll and Conán squelching behind.

A silent journey it was, for the most part, all except for one or two efforts on Fionn's part to learn what had happened in that toothroom with the druid. But he got little satisfaction.

'No, Fionn. Sorry, but he told us to tell no one about

it before Cormac's ears had heard the story first.'

Fionn grumbled, but tried again. 'At least couldn't ye show me what they look like.'

'We can't do that either,' and it seemed to him that the words were spoken through thin and close-drawn lips.

'Only at the next feast in the Hall of Tara can we let 'em be seen. Otherwise, he told us, they'd all fall out.'

This seemed most peculiar to Fionn. Why should there be such odd conditions to a job already done? But, then, he knew only too well the peculiarities of druids and so questioned no more. Yet he could not help but add, to himself, 'Better, maybe, for ye if they did fall out – after what I saw.'

But he had no wish, just then, to make difficulties. Let Taoscán do what had to be done, if anything. At least he would be able to put things right, if the worst came to the worst.

It was almost candle-lighting time when the homely shape of Tara's hill became visible, and a new spring livened their step.

'Are ye sure ye can't give me any little look at all?' he tried one last time. They did not even reply to this, only shook their heads vigorously. He shrugged. 'All right. Ye can go on up ahead. I'll call to see Taoscán. I want to have a few words with him. An' here, take this with ye. Tell Murchadha 'tis the best we could do.' He dumped the huge pike unceremoniously from his shoulders and they dragged it off up the hill.

Taoscán knew by one look at Fionn's face that all was not well.

'Come in,' he said urgently, beckoning his friend to a

seat. 'Sit and tell me what's wrong.'

Fionn seemed not to hear, for he stood in the middle of the floor, blinking, his lips moving silently.

'We found the house in Dál gCais we were looking for, all right, but I saw things there that . . . that . . . '

Taoscán looked sharply at him.

'That what? Go on. Tell me more.'

But Fionn could not continue. His voice had suddenly gone. And try as he might no effort of his could squeeze out even one more word. His hands scrabbled at his throat as his eyes began to roll wildly.

Taoscán tried to calm him.

'Easy, Fionn. Be quiet for a minute until I see – '

But Fionn appeared to be in a full-scale panic now. He began to cough and gurgle, mouthing silently all the while, scattering spits about him. Taoscán retreated to a safe distance to avoid a wetting, grabbing for several small jars as he did so. In a corner he began a furious bout of expert mixing and pouring, then held out the concoction to Fionn.

'Here! Swallow this, quick.'

No notice whatever from Fionn. He was too busy choking now, it seemed.

Only one way to handle a case like this, Taoscán knew. He snatched his spell-book – which he normally handled only with gloves – flicked it open precisely and began to chant one of his most powerful remedies, Ortha na seacht lúb. Lucky for Fionn he had such a learned friend. At once the frenzy died away and he sank to his knees, gasping for breath and still clutching his neck.

Taoscán eyed him silently for several moments. 'Now,

Fionn, tell me what it was you saw in that house.'

Fionn, breathing heavily, still on his knees, stopped. Carefully he tried to speak but a dumb animal sound was all that came. Then, as if remembering something important, his eyes opened wide and he began to gesture urgently.

'Gnnh! Mmmnu!' He struggled to his feet, to the door, dragging Taoscán with him, then jabbed at the darkness, towards Tara's palace.

When Taoscán still showed puzzlement Fionn lifted him, held him stiff-armed before him and pounded up the hill.

It was a sight the guards at the main gate had never before witnessed: the chief druid of Ireland clutched and carried as a child might carry a doll. They would surely have laughed if it had been anyone else but now they knew better. They stepped back smartly as the strange spectacle passed them at a rush. Across the yard Fionn galloped, towards the Great Hall.

And then they heard it, or rather Taoscán did.

'Stop, Fionn,' he hissed. 'This instant! Stop!'

He shuddered to a halt, toes carving ruts in the yard-dust.

'Let me down. Now! And be ready for the worst.'

Taoscán's attention was already on the feasting-hall door, and as he beckoned Fionn closer to it strange sounds met their ears, the sound of keening, pililiú-ing, weeping and slobbering. Or . . . was it laughter?'

They gaped at each other uncertainly. How could – ?

Fionn began to nod his head furiously. He opened his mouth again – and this time a mudslide of words poured out, all jumbled, all senseless.

Taoscán clapped both his hands to Fionn's cheeks, held them firmly, closed his eyes and concentrated. In that tense silence he drew up from the depths of his old mind all the magic that might free Fionn from whatever now gripped him and when at last he relaxed he whispered severely, 'No more talk! Keep quiet until I bring some meaning out of this.'

He listened intently but if he did, Fionn snatched his head away and panted, 'It has something to do with Goll an' Conán. I sent 'em on up here before me.'

Taoscán nodded, licked his lips, then opened the door an inch or two.

The sight inside was as strange as ever he had witnessed or heard, even during the busy season at Gleann na nGealt, where the oddest of the odd was normal.

'By the seven crutches of Balor, I never saw the like of this.'

He said it so faintly that Fionn knew it must be serious, indeed.

'Here, let me see,' and he lifted the old man gently aside.

Later, when telling that night's story to his son Oisín and later still to grandson Oscar, he might laugh. But not now. For at the top table King Cormac sat wailing his eyes out, shuddering with sorrow, while all around him the Fianna and the men of Iceland and Persia were doubled up, braying, whinnying with laughter.

Fionn gaped, mystified. Then suddenly, before his eyes and for no reason he could grasp, everything changed. In the very middle of a long head-back bawl, Cormac snivelled to a halt, then burst out into a gurgling chuckle. At that instant the laughter of the others stopped as if it had been chopped off. A pause. As if to draw breath. And off they went again but this time into a dark pit of crying so sorrowful and pitiful that the rafters started to vibrate and slabs of plaster began to fall from the walls. It was as if everyone related to them had died all at once.

'What in the name o' Lugh –?'

'I don't know yet,' growled Taoscán, 'but I'll soon put a finish to it.'

He was mistaken, as the rest of that night would prove, but now their attention was drawn to the hall once again, for the crying ceased suddenly. Another pause. Then mirth once more shook the room, rising, rising in waves, then falling to lunatic chuckles and giggles, while in the midst of all Cormac again began to wail his eyes out, his tears splattering on to the table and floor in spite of all his sleeves could do.

Taoscán sighed and rubbed his forehead.

'If anyone asked me, now, Fionn, I'd say someone has put these people inside under enchantment. But we'll have to go in there, whether we like it or not.'

'But if we do, won't the same thing happen to us?'

Taoscán sighed again and was silent a moment.

'Hmm! Yes. My old head is addled from it all. Look, better if I enter first, maybe. You stay here and if you see any change in me, come in quickly and bring me out. Drag me if you have to.'

Fionn nodded, and with a deep breath Taoscán pulled open the door and strode into that noisy den of lunacy.

Not a whit of notice was paid to him. Everyone was busy sobbing, shaking, thumping tables with heads and fists. It was an eerie feeling, to go unrecognised among so many friends but as he gazed around him he could see no obvious explanation for this strange behaviour. He stood a moment, looked again.

And then it happened.

Goll rose, stumbled from one of the guest places at the top table, and fell to his knees before the druid.

'Taoscán,' he pleaded, fear in his face, 'do something, quick. This place is gone mad.'

He had no sooner stared at Taoscán than the druid's eyes seemed to glaze over and a tremor shook him. And another. Then several more. And before Fionn's frightened eyes the old man was in a fit of uncontrollable hysterics, pounding his knees, doubled up.

'Heavens above, he'll have heart failure,' Fionn whispered, startled. He delayed not an instant though, flung back the door, dashed in and snatched the old man out into the corridor. There, in the dimness and silence, he shook his friend, tried to calm him.

'Taoscán! Taoscán! Stop it! What's wrong with you?'

He could feel the laughter subside as the old body grew calm again. Taoscán looked at him, a worried stare.

'Lucky for all of us you were there to pull me out of that place before the spell could work its way fully.'

'Spell! What spell? What's going on in there?'

'I'll explain that later. But now, call out Goll and Conán. And whatever else you do, don't look at their faces.' Fionn could hear the warning in the old voice. He entered the hall again, slowly, carefully, leaving Taoscán to recover outside. Goll was still kneeling, dazed, where he had made his plea to the druid. Conán was standing, his hands before his face, at the second guest place. Without another thought Fionn grabbed him, steered him towards the door and pulled Goll to his feet as they passed.

'Look away from me. That's an order!'

Taoscán was at the door.

'Get them down to my place, quick. I'll be along in a minute.'

As Fionn strode off, dragging the other two along, Taoscán ventured into the noisy hall once more, cautiously. Was this madness contagious, he wondered. No matter. He had to take that chance. Careful to look into no one's eyes directly, he faced the crowd from near the top table.

'Cease this!' he shouted.

Not an iota of notice did anyone take, then or during any of the spells he attempted, one after another, over the next fifteen minutes. And when he faltered at last, breathless, he noticed something else: that those at the tables were growing weak under the strain of their sorrow and levity. Some were already stretched among their platters and bowls, others crumpled on the floor. This was anything but fun!

He hurried from the hall, through the gaping main gates, down the hill. Fionn was waiting at the cave, a firm grip yet on his two captives.

'Hold them until I search my books, Fionn. It shouldn't take long.'

He was wrong in that, for no matter how or where he searched over the next hour – and no one in Ireland had as large a library as he – he could find nothing that answered his need. Even in smoke he could summon up no hint.

'Strange. Very odd,' he whispered. 'Something – or someone – is resisting me, for whatever reason.'

He returned to where Fionn still held Goll and Conán.

'No luck, Fionn. There's something getting in the way of my magic.'

'O'course there is!' cried Fionn. 'The druid o'Feakle, the toothman. Who else?'

At the mention of that place Taoscán stopped. Understanding seemed to dawn on him.

'Of course. That's it, for sure. Why didn't that occur to me?'

Fionn stared at him. 'I hope you're not joking, Taoscán. 'tis hardly the time for it.'

'No, Fionn, not joking. Just tired.'

He shook himself.

'Trouble is coming,' he sighed. 'Big trouble. I know it.'

'As if we hadn't enough already,' growled Fionn.

'You know nothing about trouble until you see what is about to fall on us,' said the old man wearily. 'But duty must and will be done. And with the help of the powers of Light we may come through safely.'

Just then there was a mighty banging and hullooing from the direction of the main gates above.

'By Lugh an' his mother, 'tis started already,' cried Fionn, though as he cocked his ears he paused.

'There's something about that noise I recognise,' he said uncertainly. 'Could I be dreaming, d'you think?'

'Only one way to find out, Fionn. Go up and see. I'll be right behind you.'

With a stern order to Conán and Goll not to move, he placed them in two opposite corners of the cave, faces to the wall, though as he hurried out the thought crossed his mind that it might not be a bad idea to set them face-together. At least they would keep each other busy that way!

He bounded up the hill, sword and dagger drawn, well aware that no one stood between Tara and destruction except Taoscán and himself. That he was not entirely correct in that thought events would soon show.

He was still some way from the summit when the noise from above stopped him. He *knew* that sound! And the nearer he got the more certain he became. It was . . . But how? What business would she have here now? But there could be no doubt about it. How could he ever mistake Maighnis's voice for any other!

His run trailed off into an uncertain fidgeting a few yards from the gateway. A thunderous thumping in the yard roused him and a voice raised angrily. 'Where is he? I'll damage this place if he doesn't show his face – now! Fionn! Come out, you lug!'

He groaned. Home had suddenly come to Tara, it seemed, though why this should be so he had no idea.

He shook himself, bit his lip and advanced nervously. He was still only in the gateway when he was seen, but not by his wife. She was too busy uprooting with her bare hands one of the huge oaken corner-posts of King Cormac's House. it was one of her serving-women from the Hill of Allen who first put eyes on him. And the news quickly travelled.

'He's here! The boss!'

Maighnis dropped Cormac's House with a crash of breaking furniture within.

'Boss?' she snorted. 'What boss?'

She saw Fionn. 'Who? Him?' And she sniggered.

Fionn gritted his teeth. But no sense in starting an argument here and now. More urgent matters in hand. He strode forward, noting the other women as he did so, six of them in all.

'Well, Maighnis, so ye paid us a visit, eh?'

He clapped his hands on her shoulders, as if man-to-man. She brushed him off.

'We did. I'm sick an' tired o' looking at the wall at home. Time I had a holiday, too, an' saw a bit o' this action here in Tara you're always telling us about.'

'And no better time could you have chosen,' came a quiet voice from behind her. She recognised it at once. Taoscán! She spun round, falling to one knee and bowing, all in the one movement. She could still be graceful when she wished, Fionn noted with interest. She kissed Taoscán's hand reverently.

'Long time since she did that to mine,' Fionn thought with a half-smile.

But the druid was speaking again. 'Maighnis, the gods have sent you' – and he briefly explained the predicament they were in, making sure Fionn also could hear.

'Everyone there in the hall will be worn out and useless when the Evil Thing comes, as soon as darkness falls. We'll get no help there. So, if ever you wanted to help your king and country this is the time – and you, too' he added to the other women, smiling. 'But come. First things first.'

He led them to his cave and scribbled a quick message, twice, then sealed each piece of parchment carefully.

'Maighnis, these messages must go at once to the men

named here,' – he held up the parchments. 'Without their help I can do little. Pick the two women of your choice from these six. Fionn, to His Majesty's stables, quick! Bring back two of the best horses.'

All that was done, and as the messengers galloped off with final directions and a strong blessing from Taoscán he shook his head.

'If Mogh Ruith and Fíodh Mac Neimhe are at home to do what I ask of them, we may yet get the better of the Dark.'

Fionn understood. He had met those powerful druids on a few occasions and knew what they could do. Obviously Taoscán was taking no chances with whatever it was that was coming.

As the light of evening faded into darkness Fionn was pacing up and down outside Taoscán's cave, waiting for he knew not what, stopping often to listen to the noises from Tara. Even the laughter sounded mournful and worn-out now and he feared the worst, if some help did not arrive soon . . .

Luckily assistance did arrive, and from an unexpected source. As he paused to watch the sun setting he noted a movement far to the west. He narrowed his eyes and peered. 'Taoscán,' he called. 'Come out here. There's someone coming.'

And as the old man bustled to his side he added, 'Have we anything to fear, d'you think?'

Maighnis joined them now and they stood silently watching the dim forms take more definite shape as they drew nearer. Fionn suddenly clapped his hands. 'They're ours! Isn't that Caoilte!'

And sure enough it was Caoilte Mac Rónáin, leading fifteen men of the Fianna. Fionn beckoned them urgently to him.

'What's wrong?' asked Caoilte.

'Never mind that for now,' Fionn replied. 'Are ye well armed?'

'Indeed we are. We're on our way back from trying to teach manners to the O'Connors, an' you can't do that without weapons, as you well know.'

Fionn allowed himself a little smile. The same O'Connors of Lár na hÉireann understood no kind of persuasion unless it was accompanied by weapons – either that or magic; to attempt to reason with them invited only their scorn and mockery.

There were a dozen other questions Fionn wanted answers to but they could wait. All that mattered now was that this small section of the Fianna was here, was most welcome and would surely be of help.

'Caoilte, I want these men to surround the Hill of Tara. Spread 'em out in a way that they can see each other at all times. We're expecting company shortly that mightn't be pleasant, so stay wide awake.'

Just then Taoscán added, 'Before you go, come with me a moment. More than ordinary weapons will be needed to hold back what is approaching.'

He led them back to his cave, motioned them to wait at the entrance. Only Fionn accompanied him inside and watched once again while the old man, with expert hand and eye, chose this, that and the other ingredient from his shelves, mixed them to the whispered accompaniment of ancient words that only he knew. The resulting ointment he brought carefully out.

'Now, men, quick. Show me here your weapons.'

Swords, daggers were bared, axes and clubs swung forward.

'Hold them steady now while I do what must be done.'

They did so and in the gloom Taoscán carefully rubbed on each the secret stuff of his spell, with more words, different in every single case. He was hardly finished when a clammy dampness seemed to gather at their backs.

'Here it is, men. Turn and hold your ground. But scatter out. Caoilte! Do what Fionn told you. Now is the time of testing. Keep them off while I consult my books for a cure for the men in the hall.'

He hurried away and left them to face the enemy.

They had barely clambered to their positions around the hill when the first attack broke on them, cold, horrible and organised. What exactly the creatures were that now attempted to capture the Hill of Tara was impossible to say, for they were more shadows than of solid substance. But that their intentions were no good was clear from their unfriendly movements, from the dark claws which they reached towards the defenders' throats. There was no sound, though, except the panting of the Fianna as they probed and lunged this way and that to keep the creatures back.

Fionn ran hither and thither, trying to make sure that none broke through that thin line of defenders but he could not be everywhere and it was obvious that sooner or later his men must tire. And what then? He had barely pushed that ugly thought from his mind when a hand grasped his shoulder. He leaped several feet into the air and whirled around to strike out. But it was Maighnis and her two women.

'Here, give us weapons, quick, an' we'll sort out a few o' these shadowy lads.' He gawked. Women fighting in battle? But then, why not? If ever they should, now was the time. He passed Maighnis his dagger and his spear, the Gath Dearg, then ordered the men nearest him to do likewise for the other women.

It was a wise decision, for those extra weapons in the women's strong hands made all the difference. It narrowed the gap between each defender, made a breakthrough that bit more difficult. And so they fought on, stabbing and slashing, more and more tired, until the first rays of the sun shimmered over the eastern hills.

And suddenly it was all over. The creatures vanished without trace or warning. Fionn and the others sank to their knees, panting, exhausted. But there could be no rest until Taoscán said so.

'Keep alert,' Fionn cried. 'We mightn't be done yet.'

Moments after daylight Taoscán shuffled from his doorway. He too was bleary-eyed.

'Any luck?' Fionn asked him.

'It is not a matter of luck, Fionn. There's a certain solution to every problem but this one is hidden from me yet.'

He looked about him at the weary men and women where they lay, then smiled. 'Wonderful work you all did this past night,' he beamed, but then added more soberly, quietly, 'Yet they will be back, be certain of that.'

He stared then, westward and south, muttering. Fionn,

close by him, heard his words: 'Lord Lugh, look kindly on us now. Let Fíodh and Mogh Ruith arrive in time. Before darkness, if possible, please.'

'So,' Fionn mused as he sauntered off, 'Taoscán isn't confident he can keep the creatures off by his own power. That's bad news for us.' But he kept a cheerful face and an encouraging voice.

'Rest as much as ye can,' he told his wife and friends. 'We'll need to be at our best tonight.'

But there were several things to do at once. First, the Great Hall. Taoscán and himself hurried up to see how those inside had survived the night. At the gates the guards' faces told them enough: things were not well.

They found that much out for themselves when they pushed in the door. All that greeted them was a low voiceless sobbing and wheezing, and as they stepped into the gloom – there were no candles lit now – they saw men stretched in grotesque shapes in all parts of the room but mainly under tables. Holding their throats they were, as well as their stomachs and heads. Every one of them appeared to be in the last stages of agony. Taoscán shook his head.

'It was bound to be like this. Such laughing and crying would wear out any man living.'

'But ... but can't you do something?' Fionn almost shouted. 'There's little life left in 'em. They'll die if – '

'Do you think I don't know that!' Taoscán snapped. His tone of voice quietened Fionn. 'Come on,' he said, turning quickly. 'Come down with me, this instant, to my workshop. Bring four men with you.'

By the time Fionn had chosen the four the old man was

half-way home. They caught up with him at the door and his instructions were brief.

'I have a thing inside that will save the lives of those above. It won't cure but at least they will not die – yet. And, Fionn, these two in here, Goll and Conán, take them away and remove the teeth they got in Feakle, before more harm is done. If Mogh Ruith and Fíodh were here we might be able to cancel out the spell that is in them and leave them be but now there is no time. So do it, in whatever way seems good to you.'

Fionn nodded, then told the others, 'Ye heard what he said. Follow me, an' don't look at their faces, unless ye want to be like the crowd in the hall above.'

It was a timely warning, for if anyone imagined Conán and Goll were about to agree quietly to losing their new teeth it would have been a most serious mistake. They were still in their corners, facing the wall, when Taoscán entered.

'Stay where ye are,' Fionn commanded. 'Don't stir,' and he motioned the others forward urgently.

The two brothers, when they felt themselves grasped neck and shoulders, did what they were trained to do: they fought. And no matter how Fionn ordered them to be quiet they did their very utmost to escape, to face and fight their own friends struggling to subdue them.

Finally, when it seemed that they might actually get the better of their attackers, Fionn decided that drastic action was needed. With two quick and well-aimed blows, carefully judged to do no mortal damage, his terrible left fist (that fist that had ended the conquering ambitions of Dáire Colgach and smashed to splinters the royal ship of Thorvald Trogvasson, would-be destroyer of Ireland) laid them out senseless before real harm could be done.

There was no more delay. From somewhere on his person he produced a blacksmith's pincers and gave short orders, 'Open up Goll's gob, there.'

That was done, and Fionn made quick and expert work of pulling every tooth that man possessed, new and old alike. The same grim operation left Conán slumped on the floor beside his brother.

'Here, Caoilte. Take these cursed teeth an' throw 'em as far ever as you can.'

'No. Stop!'

It was Taoscán. With a quick touch he stopped the bleeding that might otherwise have killed the brothers, then straightened up.

'Leave those teeth here. They will be needed when my two friends come. This . . . this evil is not past yet.'

Fionn stared at him.

'If they come. How do we know they ever got the messages you sent?'

'They did, Fionn. Are you doubting the women who went?'

He smiled mischievously, and Fionn recognised it as such. Instinctively he glanced around him. And sure enough, there at the door was Maighnis, head cocked, fists on hips, watching, waiting.

'Me? Doubting those fine women? I am not! They did their duty – I'm sure.' The last words, though barely whispered, brought a snort from Maighnis:

'Always the same in this miserable land.' She gritted her teeth as she said it, almost sneering. 'Men make all these troubles an' mistakes but can they get themselves – never mind us – out of 'em? Oh, no!'

Fionn was about to take her up on that, answer hotly that maybe if mothers made a better job of rearing their children, sons especially, things might be otherwise. But Taoscán saw from his face what was in his mind and raised a finger in warning.

'There's much truth in what you say, Maighnis,' he nodded reasonably. 'And the way you fought last night will be a great encouragement to women everywhere to try to change the world themselves, and not wait for men to do it for them.'

She seemed happy with this response and for the moment all was quiet again.

There was yet much work to be done, though. The search for a cure for those in the hall had to go on, as well as plans for dealing with the toothshop in Feakle. But where were Fíodh Mac Neimhe and Mogh Ruith?

'I hope they're not gone beyond the sea on some business,' Taoscán murmured as he paced outside the gate, stopping often to gaze west and south. 'I have a feeling, though, that they're not too far away.'

'Trying to reassure himself, I s'pose,' Fionn thought. Then he spoke up. 'Why can't you go ahead without 'em, Taoscán? Surely you have the power to put someone as miserable as that lad in Feakle in his place.'

'Maybe. But it is not for me alone to destroy a brother-druid. Three heads are better than one for that.'

'Maybe that's so but you saw what he tried to do to us last night. That proves he's bad-minded. What harm did we ever do him that he'd want to attack Tara like that?'

'Power,' replied Taoscán simply. 'It makes men – even the best of men – do strange, sometimes dishonourable, things.'

'Which reminds me,' Fionn added quickly, 'I never got to tell you about his cursed house of teeth. He stopped me from doing that, the devil. An' if 'tis dishonour you want to hear about, I can – '

'Another time, Fionn, I'm afraid. Look!'

There was an edge of excitement in his voice as he pointed urgently to the southwest. Fionn's eyes followed his finger. There was nothing.

'What – ?'

'Look again.'

And now he saw it, or rather them: two birds winging towards Tara. He could make out now that one was black, one white, and now that the black one seemed to be a raven, the white one a dove. No word was spoken, though several others of the Fianna now joined them, all staring at the unusual pair.

Closer and closer they came, and there was something else odd about them: in its beak the dove held a small satchel while the raven clasped another, slightly bigger, in its claws. Fionn glanced sideways at Taoscán, to ask him what this could mean. The old face was lit by a look of pure joy and relief and his arms were raised. The birds swooped once only, then landed delicately onto his upturned palms. He began to speak immediately, words of an old friend meeting longtime friends. Fionn felt almost jealous, but only for a moment. Here was the help they had been waiting for. He was sure of it.

All that followed was done in a whirl of activity:

Taoscán's hurrying to his cave, talking to the birds as he went, their several minutes behind the closed door while Fionn kept everyone else at a respectful distance, then Taoscán's stepping out again, followed closely by Mogh Ruith and Fíodh Mac Neimhe, those great men of power whom most of the Fianna and the people of Ireland knew about only by repute.

There was a burst of clapping as they emerged, which Taoscán acknowledged by a little smile.

'Fionn,' he said, 'we have work to do, serious and urgent, above.' He flicked an eye towards Tara. 'See to it that there is no disturbance or noise.'

Fionn nodded and they went at once to the Great Hall and about their task.

When the door opened two hours later it was Cormac who was first to enter the light of day. He was pale, dishevelled and obviously very weak, for as soon as he released the door jamb he staggered and almost collapsed. But not quite. Summoning up all his royal pride he steadied himself, swayed but did not fall. Slowly he looked around, like a man in a trance or very drunk, then tottered across the yard towards his private quarters – most likely to his bed.

It was a scene repeated a hundred times during the next hour and more as, one by one, painfully slowly, those who had been so near to their deaths in that hall began to live again and breathe God's fresh air.

Long before the last man had been welcomed from that building, though, the three druids were back hard at work in Taoscán's quarters, this time to settle accounts once and for all with the tooth doctor of Fiacail.

What they did within and how they did it were not for ordinary mortals to know but when at last they called Fionn into their presence Maighnis was also invited. This caused much shaking of heads among the Fianna but no one cared to question the reasoning of Ireland's three most powerful druids.

'Be seated,' Taoscán nodded as the door closed behind them. 'And listen.' He stood as he talked, the other two at either side.

'Through these' – he picked up the two bags the druids had brought and spilled out the contents: seven short hazel sticks from one, seven rowan rods from the other – 'we have found who it is that owns that house in Fiacail, though why he does what he does is yet hidden in darkness. But if it can be discovered we will do so. And though we could now sweep both him and that place of shame ('Aha!' thought Fionn, 'they found out about the heads, I'll bet') from off the face of Ireland it is better that you should do it, Fionn. You, the Fianna and also those women who fought so bravely here. And since it was women who first suggested that you visit that place for teeth, perhaps they might appreciate a chance to put things right.'

Maighnis was blushing hotly, Fionn was delighted to see, but he did not smile. Better to let it go. They would surely need to be on the best of terms if this job were to be finished successfully.

'We'll be only too glad to do what you say,' Fionn replied, 'but won't he be prepared for us? He probably knows what we're talking about this very minute.'

'No, he does not. Nor will he know of your coming until

it is too late. We have seen to that. The teeth you took from Goll and Conán allowed us to do so much.' But he explained no further, though Fionn would have loved to hear how it was done. What a tale it would make for telling on a winter night.

As it was, when they emerged he had enough to do to satisfy the curiosity of those gathered at the door, check on all those who had been stricken, pay a visit to His Highness (who was now asleep and snoring!) and then make preparations for what he hoped would be his final visit to Feakle. As evening approached he checked and double-checked with Taoscán whether they should surround Tara as on the night before but the druid was very definite.

'No, Fionn. My friends and I have very much to discover yet about Garbhán, and we – '

'About who?' Fionn interrupted.

'Ah, I forgot. The toothman. His name is Garbhán. And well named he is, too. A rough, rough person. I knew him slightly at our training school. He had big ears. That was why he was nicknamed Cluaisín. And who knows what such mockery may do to turn one's mind, though none of it is meant to be hurtful.'

'It could hardly excuse what he tried to do here against King Cormac an' Tara.'

'Nor the dishonour done to all those dead people,' added Taoscán. 'But there is more to be known yet. We have a long night's work ahead of us and while we are awake the danger to Tara is slight. So sleep. You will all need it.'

By morning all seemed back to normal at Tara. A full

night's sleep had worked wonders for men's spirits and they were raring to go. Unfortunately all who volunteered could not be accepted and it went hard with Fionn to choose the fifty warriors Taoscán had advised him he might need. Those who were disappointed – especially when it became known that Maighnis and her women were going – had to be content with a promise of future action in places yet not specified, but they knew Fionn never forgot a promise and so were resigned.

Before they left, Mogh Ruith called Fionn aside and handed him a leather bag.

'Here within is the rope – the only rope – that will hold Garbhán. Use it with care, for only once may it be used. Do him no bodily injury. Hold him for us to deal with. If we can otherwise help you we will.'

Fionn nodded. If it had been Taoscán he might have talked, questioned, but this man invited no conversation. Better to do as he said; that was all.

There was only a feeble farewell from Cormac at first as they left but Fionn assured him that whatever they might do would be for the honour and safety of His Majesty and Tara. And Cormac's handshake seemed to respond and show appreciation of that sentiment. It was warm and short, not the usual cold-fish effort that had so often set Fionn's teeth on edge.

And thus they set their faces once more for Dál gCais and Fiacail, determined that this time would be their last, the time of final settlement.

The journey as far as Loch Dearg was uneventful. There was conversation, yes, but it was short and confined to what was necessary. All minds were tense and focused on the task in hand, for no one in his correct senses could believe that an attack on a druid's house would be simple or easy.

Had they not known that they were under the protection of the three druids they would never have dared stop as they did at Cloonusker, a few miles to the east of Fiacail, to consider strategy. As they crouched there in a growing drizzle under a whitethorn bush at the edge of the pathway and listened to Fionn outline what they might or might not do when they reached the toothshop (if they could find it), each of those warriors kept his thoughts to himself.

They were nervous. That much was clear.

'I'm all for going in the front gate with twenty-five men, while the rest go over the side walls an' make so much noise that they'll think there's at least twice as many of us as there is. Has anyone a different plan?'

A brief silence. Then Maighnis pointed out something. 'Won't that druid inside be able for us no matter what way we go in?'

Fionn snorted. 'If I believed that why would I have bothered coming or asked any o' ye to come with me here at all?'

He patted the leather bag Mogh Ruith had given him.

'If only I can meet the lad in charge o' that house face-to-face I have enough here to put him in his place once an' for all. You can believe that much – as long as we're able to find our way over that last part, where we had to wear the hoods.'

That seemed to satisfy them. There was silence during several moments and much nodding. But then, as they were about to move on, Liagán stopped in the very act of rising. A listening looked gripped his face; his eyes darted this way and that. Fionn noticed it at once.

'What's the – ?'

'Shhh! Listen.'

They did. And from the deepening, dampening half-light came first a creaking and groaning, then a whumping of hooves. Every eye turned in that direction. Not a word. Not a breath.

But there it was in the gloom, louder and louder, some heavy load approaching. Fionn gestured them all into silence – as if that was necessary!

'Back! Keep back! Into the shadows, quick!' he ordered.

They were hardly out of sight when a dark shape loomed into sight: four strong horses drawing a large covered wagon, two hunched drivers, one barking occasional encouragement to the sweating animals, the other seemingly asleep. Fionn recognised at once what was there: another cargo for the toothshop. His heart jumped, he smiled coldly and the thought entered his mind that perhaps this was the druids' way of making their attack easy, making sure they found their way. Now at once he knew what could be, must be, done.

'Keep down, an' no one move until it passes,' he hissed, and no one did. When it was twenty paces or so beyond where they crouched they rose as one, fingering their weapons, but Fionn shook his head.

'Let it go on a while yet. We'll follow an' observe.'

As they crept after it they noticed once more the thread of blood it left behind.

'It'd be hard to lose track o' that,' said Maighnis,

disgusted, and those close by nodded their distaste.

For more than a mile they followed it, then Fionn decided it was time to intervene.

'Take three men, Diarmaid, an' catch hold o' the right backshaft. I'll do the same for the left one. Liagán, pick six men an' block the road ahead. Make sure the drivers don't escape to that cursed toothhouse to warn 'em. We'll give ye a few minutes to get there before we start back here.'

As Liagán slipped off, beckoning men to him as he went, Fionn said quietly to the others, 'Be getting ready. There could be hard fighting at the house – or maybe none at all, who knows.'

Wise leader that he was he wanted no one to feel left out. And even Maighnis found no fault with what he did or said.

Moments later, as the driver, tired and cold, was ordering on the horses in his usual bored half-grunt, the cart stopped so suddenly that he and his companion were sent sprawling onto the backs of the two rear horses. As they tumbled awkwardly to the ground, steel-hard arms were clamped about their necks. It was Liagán and friends.

'Not a sound,' he growled dangerously. 'The slightest move an' ye're dead men.' The two gaped goggle-eyed at the crowd now emerging from the shadows round about. They were even more frightened to see that some of their attackers were women. After a few brief questions Fionn decided that they knew little, could be of only small help.

'Tie 'em up securely,' he ordered. 'An' see that they're guarded.'

He pondered then a moment. How best to use this

wagon and cargo? He called Diarmaid, Conán and Maighnis aside.

'Any advice?' he said shortly.

The men shrugged but Maighnis, always practical, spoke up.

'Empty what's in that wagon, an' let twenty men get into it. You drive it, Fionn. Take the driver's cloak an' Diarmaid that other lad's. When they open the gates it should be something to see the look on their faces.' And she chuckled.

'As good a plan as any,' Fionn agreed and was about to instruct the men accordingly when Maighnis called him back.

'What if there's a password?'

He stopped. 'Good thinking.' Then he called Liagán to him.

''Ask the driver – nicely, mind – if there's a password at the gate.'

Liagán returned moments later, two cloaks over his arm, and nodded.

'There is. An' a strange one too.'

They waited, while he sniggered.

'Well?' growled Fionn impatiently.

'It's . . . it's . . . "My Own Toothless Mother At Home" – an' you have to sing it.'

'So, they think 'tis a big joke, do they? Before this night is over we'll see who's smiling,' and he gritted his teeth angrily.

Under Goll's direction the wagon was quickly untackled, heeled up and so emptied of its horrible contents.

Fionn addressed the men then, while most of them

were still speechless at what they had just witnessed.

'This is asking a lot, I know, but I want twenty of ye to get into that wagon there, where those heads were, while myself an' Diarmaid drive it to the gates an' get it inside that cursed place. Then ye can show what men o' the Fianna think o' low work like this,' – and he gestured towards the heap of heads.

A few hands went up first, then more and more until it seemed that everyone was willing.

'Good,' he smiled. 'But who'll remain behind to make sure that no more dishonour is done to these ... these misfortunate things. I don't want the creatures o' the forest dragging 'em away.'

Maighnis stepped forward. 'We will,' and he knew she was speaking for the other women as well as herself. He was touched.

'Thanks,' he said quietly, and men stepped back in respect, not envying them their grisly vigil.

'Liagán,' Fionn said, as Diarmaid chose the men for the wagon, 'divide the rest into two groups an' surround the house. There's a gate at the back, too. I'll leave it to yourself to do what has to be done. You'll hear the noise we'll be making inside, anyway. I'll guarantee that much.'

Liagán grinned, went about his business, and Fionn turned to the cart. All was ready. He climbed aboard, pulled the cloak about him, urged the horses forward and waved a little farewell to the women.

There was no sign of life as they approached the main gates. Fionn was pleased. The nearer they got without being challenged the better their chances.

'But, by Crom,' he thought, 'if the guards at Tara were

as slack as this I'd have 'em out for a month counting blades o' grass.'

There was still no sound when they finally trundled to a halt and Fionn was about to give the order to smash the gates when a face appeared over the battlements.

'Stop! Who's there?'

'Us,' growled Diarmaid.

'Give the password!' the guard barked, and Diarmaid sang out 'My Own Toothless Mother At Home' without even a smile, though there were several sniggers from the wagon. Fionn had to admire the coolness of the man.

The face disappeared and moments later they heard chains clanking, a large metal bar being drawn back. Then one after the other the gates creaked open and they rolled in.

Fionn's eyes darted here and there. The guards were in their usual hut, their torches flickering, but there was no one else in the yard. He nodded under his cloak and urged the horses towards the door to that room of horrors. Half-way across Diarmaid tapped the board behind him three times, and those inside readied themselves for a sudden bursting-forth.

Then ahead that ugly door opened and out filed the white-cloaked ones.

'Our reception is waiting anyway,' Fionn snarled but just then he noted something else: a slight movement to the right overhead on the balcony.

'Well, well! Look who's here. Our very own host himself.'

Diarmaid glanced up but said nothing, though he saw the tall man leaning down, eyeing them closely.

'Right!' shouted Fionn as one of the robed ones grasped the bridle, 'Out, men! We're here!'

He leaped down, sword and dagger ready, and dashed for the stairs. Whatever had to be done below Diarmaid and the others would see to. His work lay above.

He swept the two guards aside as if they were straws, bounded up the stairs five steps at a time, and arrived just as a door nearby clicked shut. He noted the slight movement.

'Ha,' he hissed, fingering Mogh Ruith's bag as he advanced carefully. 'Now we'll find out whose power is the strongest.'

But he was too experienced a soldier to rush recklessly in after such a man as Garbhán, especially in his own house.

Standing a little to one side of the door jamb he thumped firmly on the door with his foot.

'D'you want to come out, now – or will I come in?'

No response.

There could be some ugly surprise awaiting him, he knew, but 'keep your enemy in sight at all times' was a rule he had always practised. And he certainly was not about to *beg* the man inside to surrender. So, without more talk or warning he swung round suddenly and with all his strength concentrated into his left shoulder he sent the door crashing in around the floor in pieces.

As he stood there snorting, taut, armed and ready he was taken aback to find Garbhán's back to him and that man gazing calmly, it seemed, out the window. There was a moment's silence. Then the druid turned – and smiled. It was more a crooked leer, though, and when he spoke his words were low and menacing.

'I was expecting you, Mac Cumhail. You're as pre-dictable as your father and every bit as stupid.'

If any other man had said it he would have torn him to pieces but Fionn kept calm now.

'If you think I care a tráithnín for your insults you're very mistaken. I'm here to do His Highness's business, an' I will. Simple as that. So will you come peacefully or will I have to drag you?'

'Simple words, simple mind,' snarled Garbhán. 'And just as well, maybe, that you came in this way. Now I need feel no regrets for making an example of you.'

Though Fionn felt nervous now (for it was no small thing to take on a druid) he tried not to show it. But he did wish that Diarmaid or someone else would join him – quickly.

'Getting frightened, are you?' Garbhán jeered. 'I don't blame you. Because the lesson you will learn here this night – '

'If there's any lessons going to be learned 'tis you'll learn 'em,' Fionn interrupted. 'Lay your eyes on what I have here for you,' and stabbing his sword into the floor he held up Mogh Ruith's bag. 'If you have any power at all you should know what's in this.'

Slowly, carefully, he undid the thong which bound it, then drew out the rope – bright as silver – which Mogh Ruith had told him of.

Garbhán's eyes at once fastened on this strange thing. He had become deadly silent.

'I see you recognise it,' Fionn whispered as the other began to back away. No reply.

'Well, you know what I'm going to do with it now, don't you?' and he stepped carefully across the threshold into the room. But that single step seemed to break the rope's spell of fascination. Hate and fear leaped into Garbhán's face. His eyes darkened and he raised his arms as if to hurl something invisible.

Fionn in the instant of danger could think of nothing other than to fling the rope. As it whirled towards him, Garbhán tried to duck, but too late: that glittering thing seemed to have taken on a life of its own. First one end of it, then the other snaked and looped themselves about his neck, and though his fingers grasped and scrabbled to free himself, it coiled tight, then tighter, until his eyes began to pop, then glaze over, and his knees buckled under him. Fionn leaped forward, grasped him by the shoulders and held him up. But he could do little more.

Whether he would have dared cut the rope to save this man's life was never put to the test, for just then a voice thundered out behind him:

Stad den tactadh, cara mo chroí;
lig beo é fós do chúirt an dlí.

It was Mogh Ruith. And immediately the rope relaxed its hold but only enough to allow Garbhán to breathe. It kept its grip, ready to squeeze again if told.

Fionn, squinting, blinking this way and that, was still trying to take in this abrupt change in affairs when the sight of Taoscán entering the room brought a huge gasp of relief from him. And there too was Fíodh and Diarmaid.

'How could – ? Where – ?'

Taoscán, easy, friendly, laughed at Fionn's confusion. 'Everything is as it should be,' he said simply.

'Diarmaid,' Fionn muttered, 'what's happening out-side?'

'Nothing, Fionn. All finished.'

He wanted to question more but thought better of it and only nodded, bemused.

'I'll ... ah ... take a walk in the air while ye're settling up in here. If ye have no objection, that is.'

'None at all,' said Mogh Ruith briefly and led by Diarmaid, Fionn exited shakily. Outside there were no signs of destruction. All the guards, servants and tooth-room workers had been herded to one side of the yard but no blood seemed to have been spilt. Fionn scratched his head.

'How did Taoscán an' his friends arrive?' he asked.

'I can't tell you that,' replied Diarmaid. 'One minute they weren't there, next thing they were. That's all I know.'

Fionn nodded. Had they flown as birds? Or as ... ? What did it matter now? They were here and all would surely be well.

And it was. Under the close supervision of the three druids the load of heads was brought in and a hole dug in the yard. That was quickly filled with water by an extraordinary thundershower specially summoned out of the darkness by Taoscán for that purpose. Then the black cloud was thanked and dismissed, and the heads were carefully placed in the water by the toothroom workers, under threat that if they did not show every mark of respect as they did so their own heads would also be there. The water was then frozen solid by three secret words, one from each druid. If ever proof were needed of the power of those men this was surely it.

No one spoke until Taoscán said, mildly, 'There they will remain until those near and dear to them have been found. There will be grief then but gladness too.'

That too came to pass, and though, as Taoscán predicted, there were many tears shed at sight of those poor bodiless heads, great was the praise throughout the land for the Fianna and for King Cormac, a thing that pleased His Highness well. Taoscán refused to allow his own name to be mentioned at all.

'As for this house, and what will befall it, we leave that decision to King Cormac. The rest,' – and he stared hard at Garbhán – 'is for us to remedy.'

It was a remedy that Garbhán had no relish for: to be marched back to Tara, the rope round his neck, a public spectacle to all who crowded out along the way to stare. And his humiliation did not end there, for he still had to be tried in public at Tara before nine druids, 'so that all may see that no one is above the law,' as Taoscán put it to King Cormac. He was conveyed to the royal dungeons, the rope still in place, and warned solemnly that any attempt to escape would only bring about his death.

Perhaps that would have been the best ending, had he had the sense to attempt it.

At that night's feast the hall was buzzing with excitement, partly because Taoscán's two distinguished guests were present, and also because a story was in the air: what those wise ones had discovered about Garbhán's desire to capture Tara.

When all the eating had been done, wine, mead and

uisce beatha were brought forth and the guests settled to listen. Taoscán stood briefly, curtsied and began.

'If it causes offence to no one, I will sit as I speak.'

There was no objection to that. He continued, 'That man – one of our brother druids, I regret to say – whom you saw led in today and lodged in the dungeon, has betrayed great trust and will assuredly be punished. No doubt you all know by now the nature of his deeds – indeed many of you have seen it with your own eyes. And why, I hear you ask, would one who had so much and who was sworn to do good, turn his back on the Light and face instead the Dark? An answer to that would reveal the very nature of man. Even we can only guess at it. But we have discovered why he went about his evil business in the fashion he did.'

Men hunched themselves forward to miss no word – as did Maighnis and her women – and over the next hour and more he unfolded the details of a peculiar tale. He told of how Garbhán, not content to gather herbs, work spells and cure ills, push back the Darkness with the light of his druid's knowledge, had wanted much, much more – and quickly, too. He had decided to go to Craglea and demand (no less!) that Aoibheall, the Wise One, grant him the wisdom of the Otherworld. She had pitied him his foolishness and received him kindly. But when she explained to him that such wisdom must be earned by patience and long study he returned her the bitter word.

His listeners goggled at such impertinent stupidity and more than one of them thought to ask how such a man could ever have become a druid of Ireland, but they hesitated to interrupt Taoscán.

'But she was kind to him – if kindness is the word for it. She gave him a little part of the power he asked for, in the form of the ability to replant teeth. In the hands of a wise man it could have brought great joy into the world. But for Garbhán it was a means of avenging himself on the world for imagined insults and slights. Especially against Tara, where he felt he should be working and to which he had not been called. Now that skill, her gift, has been his ruin.'

'What's to be done with the villain?' interrupted Cormac sombrely.

'Tomorrow his sentence will be pronounced when our colleagues arrive. I have sent for them, never fear. But the fate of that house of dishonour at Fiacail is in your hands, Cormac.'

'An' if you want it pulled down, or burned, there isn't a man here who wouldn't be proud to have a hand in it, Your Majesty,' added Fionn.

Cormac nodded wisely. 'I'll make up my mind in the quiet hours of the night,' he said. 'But be certain that not a stone of it will be left standing or ever be used for building again.'

And the odd thing was that he seemed to mean every word he said. But a crafty, distant look had entered his eye. And Taoscán noted it. There was something else brewing, though what it was he could not yet tell.

Next day, early, the other six druids began to arrive. Even the most careless or stupid of those who saw them coming realised that something serious was afoot, for such a gathering of the wise had not been seen at Tara since Galar had been banished to the oak-roots in the notorious case of the Dream Hour.[1] They entered hard-faced, with neither smile nor greeting for anyone.

'Aha!' whispered Goll to Conán, 'they know what people are thinking. If proper justice isn't done here today their name is dirt, an' don't worry, they'll protect themselves.'

'True for you,' Conán nodded. 'Garbhán is in for a hard time of it, I'd say.' Goll could there and then have told the story of Éimhear MacCriotha as proof that druids were not always as upright and honest as they were expected to be but why bother? Everyone knew it anyway; they were only human, no matter how their great education and power sometimes made it seem otherwise. Yet expectations would continue as they always had; people needed to believe that certain things in this ever-changing world were firm and secure.

In the Great Hall there was hardly room for those present to scratch themselves. Before the trial even got under way it was obvious that many people would be carried out unconscious or worse if some change was not speedily made. Yet still the people were gathering in their hundreds outside the gates, clamouring to be admitted. To avoid injury and disappointment and to spread the message of justice as widely as possible, Taoscán suggested to Cormac that the trial be moved to outside the walls, in fact to the bright southern slope of the Hill of Tara. His Majesty had no objection so long as 'our noble person is observed and our royal justice is seen to be done'.

Taoscán made quite sure that both those conditions were met, and so the trial began, watched by a multitude of people larger than ever turned out to see the Tailteann

Games, a crowd beyond the powers of even scholars to count.

When all was settled and the people were quiet Mogh Ruith rose. By his druid's power he made quite sure that everyone could hear him.

'There will be no interruptions, no laughter, no noise at all while this trial is in progress. At another time no one would be present while we examined the accused one. But this once may you witness what true justice is.'

There was little fear of disorder. The opposite, in fact. All those present were more than conscious that they were witnessing a thing their grandchildren would be privileged to hear of.

There was not a sound as Garbhán was led out, still bound. He cast poisonous glares on those about but Taoscán ignored this as he said heavily, 'You have done – the witnesses are there to show it – what cries to Lugh for vengeance. We already know your deeds and the manner in which you did them. All that remains is to decide your punishment. But if you wish to repent . . . perhaps . . . '

The crowd was listening attentively for the reply. They were not disappointed.

'Punishment? Repent? Before ever these people hear anything of how I have been treated? Is that not pre-sumption of the lowest order? Of what am I guilty? Trying to better myself? Trying to make fat and useless Tara notice that there are other ways of looking at this world than those *you* think are normal?'

Every eye turned to Cormac to see what his reaction would be to this insolence but he was picking his nose and seemed not to have heard. People nodded. At least something was still normal.

Garbhán continued, disgust in his voice, 'I have nothing to answer here. You, my so-called judges' – he spat in their direction – 'have the power but no authority to pronounce a sentence on me. And even if you do it will avail you nothing.'

He smirked, and the crowd, astonished at this effrontery, looked at the judges for fire and immediate destruction. But there was only steel-eyed silence. Taoscán and his friends were obviously prepared to let him condemn himself by his own words. He proceeded to do so.

'I will not accept whatever charges you bring against me. They are false. You fool yourselves to think I will submit to you and your prattling about justice.'

'Why don't ye shut him up, Taoscán?' asked Fionn angrily. 'Take away his voice, as he tried to do to me. Letting him go on like this is only giving bad example to all these people.'

Taoscán stroked his beard and seemed about to take Fionn's advice when Mogh Ruith sprang to his feet.

'Silence, wicked one! Cease this babble. Your guilt is not in doubt. Only your sentence. And in that you are fortunate that your rank gives you a choice.'

He looked at Taoscán and the other druids. One by one they nodded.

'Your choice is this and no other: do you wish, like Galar, to be confined in the oak tree's roots for seven generations or will you take your chance again with Aoibheall at Craglea?'

Garbhán laughed and was about to launch into another attack when Taoscán pointed at him and warned.

'Make your choice. You have seven words – only seven words – left in which to do so. Else we will choose for you.'

Garbhán knew that this was the end of the road. He stared a vicious stare at each of his judges in turn as if to say: 'Somewhere, somehow again we will meet and then will be the true reckoning of our accounts.'

When he spat out his answer it was a single word: 'Craglea.' And he sneered.

'Very well. Craglea let it be,' were Taoscán's final words to him. 'Fionn, see to it that he is delivered there, left at that exact place, Carraig Aoibheall, secured with that same rope.'

Fionn nodded and led Garbhán, still bound, still defiant, back to the dungeon, much to the delight of everyone present.

But all was not finished yet. Taoscán faced the crowd. 'It still remains for those bloody ones who served him to be punished also. But that we leave to King Cormac's breitheamhs. They will see to it that none of the guilty escape.'

He sat then and after a last hurried consultation between himself and the other eight druids they rose, bowed to Cormac and withdrew, their work done. Shortly afterwards the king himself retired behind the walls of Tara and the crowd began to scatter, with much to consider after their day's 'entertainment'.

The rest of the daylight hours were hectic ones for Fionn. A secure escort had to be arranged for Garbhán to Craglea but there was no difficulty in that. In fact there were more volunteers than were needed, and the six finally chosen (which included Goll and Conán, of course) were given into Diarmaid's capable command.

Then a huge feast in honour of the visiting druids had to be prepared and though Murchadha Maor organised matters within the walls it was left to Fionn to muster enough men to capture, at short notice, the game necessary for such an occasion – no small task since Murchadha's order was for thousands of everything, as usual.

That feast was scheduled to last three nights, long enough to allow Garbhán to be delivered to his fate and those escorting him to report back, for fear of any mishaps. And during the first night, of course, all talk was about the man below in the dungeon, his family and ancestors, his motives and a hundred other matters related to him and his doings.

On the second night, while Diarmaid and the escort were leading their prisoner to Craglea, it continued the same way unabated. But there was one person surprisingly absent on that night: Taoscán.

That morning, when Diarmaid had been about to collect Garbhán from his cell, Taoscán was there before him.

'Diarmaid,' he said, 'think it no impertinence or lack of trust in you, but I have decided to come with you to Craglea. I wish to witness for myself how Aoibheall responds to what has happened. Are you agreeable?'

Diarmaid knew that the old man was being pleasant, mannerly, attempting to spare his feelings. For the truth was that he could come if he wished, without even asking.

'Of course,' he replied. 'We'd be more than glad to have you.'

And as they marched away from Tara he confided to Taoscán in a low voice. 'To tell the truth, I'm relieved you're here. I wasn't exactly sure if there were special things that had to be done when Garbhán was being left at Craglea. The last thing I'd want is for him to escape because of something I did or didn't do.'

Taoscán smiled. 'Worry no more about it. I will make sure all is done properly.'

As they neared Craglea evening was already gathering round them but there was no stopping until they stood at the foot of Craglea Hill, looking up at the huge grey rock named after her who made it her home in this world: Carraig Aoibheall.

Garbhán, who had been silent for many miles, now began gibing, sneering once more.

'When morning comes, Mac Liath, you'll see a different side to me. I promise you that all those old fools who allowed me to make the choice I did will regret it. I'll destroy not just Tara but every one of the nine of you, no matter how long it takes me . . . ' And on and on.

'Will I strike him?' protested Diarmaid, outraged that such insults should be offered to a kind man like Taoscán.

'No need, Diarmaid. Aoibheall is listening to every word he speaks. She will see that justice is done, never fear.'

The six strong men bundled him up then to the rockface itself, where Taoscán made sure that Mogh Ruith's rope was securely in place. There he produced a rope of his own, bound Garbhán's feet with it and tied the other end to an ancient, gnarled whitethorn bush that clawed its way from a crack in the rock – Aoibheall's doorway, as he explained to Diarmaid.

'Now, let us withdraw and allow Aoibheall to show her will.'

'An' if she lets him go won't we be in danger?'

'The choice is hers to do as she thinks fit.'

They climbed down, followed by more insults from Garbhán, and camped at a respectful distance. There, while they cooked their meat in a fulacht fiadha, they could still hear him cursing. Taoscán shook his head sorrowfully.

'If he had any sense,' said Diarmaid, ''tis his prayers he'd be saying, wouldn't you think.'

'Yes,' Taoscán sighed. 'But some people learn only when their last moments are staring them in the face. And by then it is usually too late.'

They dozed many times that night, but never quite slept. Always they were expecting some great ending, a shriek, shouting or sounds of a terrible combat. But there was nothing, not even Garbhán's voice any more.

Finally, as day dawned, Taoscán rose, stretched and pointed to the rock.

'Time to see that all is as it should be – though I have no doubt it is.'

'We'll come with you, just in case,' and they all scrambled after him, wondering at how lively he could be for his years.

There was no immediate sign of Garbhán at the bush but as they drew closer every eye was drawn to the crack in the rock. There, in all the distorted gestures of one trying desperately to prevent himself being dragged into that narrow place, crouched a human skeleton. They gaped, utterly silent.

Taoscán fell to his knees, whether to pray or to examine it more closely they could not tell. One by one they looked at each other, lips dry, fingers twitching.

'Diarmaid,' said Taoscán at last, and again there was sorrow in his voice, 'these bones must be brought back to Tara for proper burial, even though many may say he does not deserve it.'

'But how do we know 'tis him? Couldn't this be a trick to put us astray?' Conán was examining the skull now.

'I don't think 'tis any trick, Diarmaid. Look at this.'

He pointed to the gold teeth.

'They're the ones we saw when we met him at the toothhouse. I'd know 'em anywhere.'

'There is Mogh Ruith's rope and mine also,' Taoscán pointed to where they were still firmly in place around the bones. That ended the argument. A hunting sack was handed over by one of the men ('expecting a bit of a chase, I was') and the bones were delicately dropped in, one by one, a job Taoscán did himself.

They turned to go then, after a short speech by Taoscán to the rock in a language they could not understand.

'Thanking Aoibheall he is, surely,' whispered Diarmaid, and the others could only agree.

But they had gone hardly a hundred paces when Taoscán stopped them.

'I must go to Fiacail,' he said. 'Go on ahead to Tara and tell Cormac what you have seen. And make no delay, for I will not be long behind you.'

They offered to accompany him, but no; what he had to do he must do alone. That much they understood, for the work of druids was often of that nature, and so they parted.

Shortly afterwards Taoscán stood in the doorway of the now-silent toothroom. There was no sound, nothing moving anywhere. As he surveyed the three tables, dark now with dried blood, his face also darkened.

'That anyone would do what you did here, Garbhán, makes me fear for men. You deserved everything that happened you last night. A pity it did not come sooner.'

The pile of broken skulls was still inside the door, a cloud of flies buzzing round it. He quickly sent them packing.

'We should have done something about these earlier,' he sighed, 'but better late than too late, I suppose.'

Then he surveyed the frozen heads in the yard, said a prayer and moved on to where the teeth were in their containers. These he examined with the utmost care, putting a few aside.

Finally, when all was done he made his way to the dún of the chief of Dál gCais. He was recognised immediately and received with ómós, as befitted his rank. He explained briefly all the recent happenings at Fiacail and men paled as they listened. He requested the chief to see that the toothshop was guarded and nothing removed – 'Anything from that place will bring misery and misfortune on him who takes it.' He could, of course, have ensured all this through his own strong magic but it was better that these people should be responsible for at least some of what concerned themselves; he would not always be here to protect them.

He waited long enough to see the guards in place and

then left at once for Tara, promising a speedy return.

Indeed Diarmaid and the others – the bag of bones held out on a long pole – had hardly arrived at Tara and begun explaining the doings at Craglea to the throng that surrounded them when Taoscán strode up the hill and called a halt, explaining that King Cormac and the eight druids had to hear it first, that grave decisions had to be made for the safety and benefit of Ireland.

'But have no fear,' he added as a mutter of disappointment spread. 'All will be revealed to you shortly. And believe me, it is a story worth the wait.'

In the quiet of Cormac's private chambers – newly repaired after Maighnis's efforts! – every detail of Garbhán's gruesome end was mulled over by the druids and all of them agreed with Taoscán that Aoibheall's patience had finally run out. The bag of bones was solid proof of that. Mogh Ruith had even a strong opinion on what was probably happening to the stupid dead one at that very moment: 'She is feeding him, bit by bit, to her dogs.'

'I hope so,' added Cormac. 'I'll give Fionn his orders this very day to take as many of the Fianna as he needs and see to it that that house is cleared off the face of my land. But before that's done, I want to see it for myself.'

'Maybe it is a visit we should all make,' said Fíodh Mac Neimhe. 'It is good for one to witness how men can sometimes sin.'

That much was agreed by all and after telling of these strange events during that night's feast, excited preparations were made over the next two days for the royal progress. Speedy messengers were sent ahead so that the chief of Dál gCais would have labourers enough ready for the work of demolition. At last they began their journey, accompanied by the king's personal scribe, Mac Cleite, with a large supply of vellum, for this was a royal event that must be recorded for all future generations.

Also brought along was the bag containing Garbhán's bones.

It was a slow progress, for every prince and chief along the route came out to greet their royal master and dozens of feast invitations had to be politely refused or postponed. But no one took offence, since it was obvious to all from the presence of the nine druids, that serious and urgent business was in hand.

When they arrived in Fiacail the chief of that country was waiting, together with the workers who had been requested, and when the welcoming formalities were complete they marched to the house of Garbhán without more delay.

It was as Taoscán had left it, silent, menacing. At first only Cormac, the druids, Fionn, Diarmaid and the chief were allowed inside.

As they were led by Fionn, wordless and wondering, throughout the house they were at first inclined to admire its scope, its furnishings and the design but as soon as they saw the frozen heads, then the toothroom with its skulls, tables and iron implements, the wonder changed to anger and disgust. When they had looked their fill it was the chief of Dál gCais who spoke first.

'Never did I realise that this was the way things were here. I only heard about the fine work he was doing, keeping people happy, an' paying his taxes. I never even thought to see for myself ... He was a druid, you see.'

He stopped suddenly, with glances of embarrassment at the druids round about him.

'No need to stop,' said Taoscán mildly. 'You say right.'

'What I'll do now, though, to make up for it,' said the chief, 'is level this place, if that's what's required.'

Cormac nodded but as they withdrew he gave orders that the crowd outside be allowed to file through, to see the horrors of the place for themselves.

The king and his group went for refreshments to the chieftain's dún, and as they sat quietly Taoscán explained why Garbhán had needed so many teeth. From his pocket he reached a handful of those he had collected on his previous visit and scattered them on a table. He stared at them.

'Only one in perhaps a thousand of these is suited to the kind of evil spells he was intent on.'

'But why should one tooth be more suited than another?' It was Diarmaid who asked it.

Taoscán shook his head. 'Family, the exact hour of a person's birth, how he died, what he ate – it is a complicated mixture requiring deep knowledge in him who would know it. But now what matters most is that they are given respectful burial, together with the heads and skulls.'

The other druids nodded.

When they returned later to Garbhán's house and all those who wished to see had done so, orders were given that all the human remains be collected together. A grave was dug at a pleasant site in the woods some distance away and all were buried with prayers for their rest, but not before Mogh Ruith had commanded that Garbhán's bones be included with them. This caused some surprise.

'Why should he have that honour?' Cormac asked angrily.

Taoscán's reply showed that perhaps there was less honour in it than might appear.

'Let him meet face to face with those he has wronged. Accounts are settled soonest that way.'

The very prospect gave those who heard those words cause to shudder on Garbhán's behalf.

Work on the destruction and levelling of the house began at once and though the workers to do the job were many it was no easy task, for it had been well built of the best materials, accompanied by many ingenious spells. It was for this reason that Taoscán insisted that a druid be always present during each of the days that the work was in progress, seven in all.

'The devil alone knows what ugly surprise might be waiting within those walls for the unwary,' was his explanation, and no one doubted the wisdom of what he said.

When all the stones had been thrown down Cormac gave orders that they be broken up, and the chief of Dál gCais had men with hammers on hand to do just that. Meanwhile the furniture, doors, gates and all else that would burn was flung into a huge bonfire whose flames reached higher than the trees all round. That, the noise and the pall of dust from the stone-breaking drew crowds of people to witness this violent end to Garbhán's evil ambitions but there was no cheering, no clapping, only the silence of wonderment.

As a huge mound of chippings grew out of the broken

stones Cormac watched it intently and on the sixth day, when work was almost completed, he called the chief of Dál gCais to him.

'I am well pleased at how all has been performed here. And to show my pleasure I intend to mend the unfortunate ... ah ... misunderstanding between Our Royal self and Craiftine Ó Dubhraic. Send for him. I would speak with him.'

The chief bowed himself out of the royal presence, smiling, but he now had a serious problem on his hands and well he knew it. For Craiftine, it was widely known, had for years refused to pay honour, respect or taxes to anyone, even to Cormac or his father before him. Most people had been content to ignore the insult and let him be, since he was reputed to be a great enchanter, especially by means of fairy music, and many attacks on his strong crannóg in Loch a' Leamhnachta on the western side of Loch Dearg had failed miserably in mysterious circumstances.

No one seriously expected him to answer the summons but encouraged, perhaps, by a written promise from Taoscán that there would be no threat to his safety, he came – more curious to see the fate of Garbhán's house, it was said, than to submit.

Cormac was all smiles, hugs and handshakes for this man he had never previously had a good word for.

'We welcome you heartily, Chief Ó Dubhraic, and it does our hearts good to see your noble face.'

Craiftine said nothing, only smiled in return, but eyed shiftly the proceedings around him, unused to this kind of greeting. Cormac personally led him about, explaining this and that detail of Garbhán's villainy, then finally coming to the point as they stood before the huge pile of chippings, which was still being added to by the sweating hammermen.

'I have heard of late that floods in Loch Dearg have done great destruction to the secret causeway to your crannóg in Loch a' Leamhnachta.'

Craiftine nodded, for that had indeed happened, making night-journeys to his island home almost impossible. Several incautious men, the worse for drink, had already disappeared and not been found. But how did Cormac know this? That was what worried Craiftine.

'Listen closely to me, then,' Cormac continued. 'Here before your eyes you see enough stones to build a road across Loch Dearg itself, if that were needed. My gift to you now – and let everyone here witness it! – is that you may take away as many loads as are necessary not alone to repair your causeway of rotten worn-out wood but to build a new one of stone fit for a king. Get horses, get carts and men; see to it yourself. And to prove to any persons of evil or suspicious mind that there is no vile or treacherous intent, none but those you wish to be present will be there to see it built, so the secret of its course may be yours alone.'

It was an offer that was loudly applauded by all those who heard it made and even Craiftine had to agree that it was nobly said.

They spent that night in talk, song and drink in the fort of the chief of Dál gCais, the best of friendship restored. Or so it seemed.

By the following noon the horsecarts had begun to

arrive and the task of transporting the chippings began. At about the same time Cormac, Fionn and the others started back to Tara after strict orders had been given by His Highness that several large loads of the chippings were to be sent on after them. They were needed at Tara, Cormac said, but he declined to explain further. Taoscán noted all this and scratched his head. Later he confided to Fionn as they made their way eastwards.

'I have a feeling there is something rotten somewhere, Fionn. I never knew Cormac to be so agreeable to an enemy before.'

'I noticed that myself,' Fionn mused. 'But who knows? He'd often surprise you, Cormac would.'

'I still think there must be a catch in it somewhere for someone.'

Taoscán was right, as usual. For no sooner was Craiftine's new causeway completed and declared open with great fanfare than something odd was noted: all those who had come to the crannóg for the great feast of celebration, as soon as they entered the gateway, felt their jaws begin to ache. Soon they were in the throes of violent toothaches, and the feast ended in disorder.

After that, every day that passed brought suffering to all and any who set foot on the new road until men refused to travel there at all and Craiftine was left alone. Eventually he had to abandon his home entirely and when he sought a site for a replacement crannóg Cormac sent firm orders that no such thing was to be permitted. He must build on the shore 'like any normal human being.' The truth, of course, was that now, if his insolence should ever return, he would be easy to subdue.

And the lesson was not lost on others. Word quickly spread of what Cormac had done, and though some criticised his actions as 'low' and 'unkingly' others chuckled and gave him full credit for being a wise politician. 'He got the better of his enemy, didn't he, an' not a drop o' blood spilt. What more could you ask for than that?'

Taoscán shook his head.

'I knew he had something up his sleeve that night before the trial.'

But it was too late to do much about it now.

'Tell me, though,' Fionn asked Taoscán, puzzled; 'how did he know there was that kind o' power in the stones?'

It was some time before his friend replied, but when he did Fionn knew that he too was mystified. All he could say was 'Sometimes kingship bestows strange and un-expected powers.'

The fact that there were several loads of the same chippings held at Tara now, a kind of secret weapon that was no secret at all, made other chiefs think twice before rebelling against Cormac – especially since he 'let slip' at almost every feast the friendly warning, 'The same could happen to anyone else too if we scatter even the dust of these on his roads.'

It made for an unusual peace in Ireland, whatever the rights or wrongs of it and for that reason Taoscán and the other druids were unwilling to condemn it outright, though they did warn Cormac that he should not use it without consulting them first.

Before Mogh Ruith, Fíodh Mac Neimhe and the rest left Tara for their own homes and business they offered Goll and Conán a new, safe set of teeth each, to replace those knocked out by Fionn, but they would have none of it.

'We'll stay the way we are,' said Goll. 'It might be awkward for a while but we'll get used to it.'

And so they did. And all the other men of Ireland who had been worried about their teeth took their example to heart. 'What's good enough for the men o' the Fianna is good enough for us, an' let the women think whatever they like.'

There was one other result of all this that no one could have foreseen: a heavy and sinister presence might have been lifted from the Dál gCais country, but the more the people of that place talked about Garbhán the more a twisted kind of pride in his doings grew up. 'Wasn't he the clever man, though, in spite of all, to make the whole of Ireland take notice of us!'

And from there began to develop a confidence in that unimportant little tribe that would, centuries later, bring the High Kingship of Ireland to them in the person of Brian Boru.

Yet if anyone, even the wisest druid, had foretold such a thing in the days of King Cormac and Fionn he would have been laughed to scorn as an idiot and a simpleton.

But in such unforeseen ways does time bring all things to completeness at last.

How Spitting Became an Art in Ireland

In these strange times of ours much is talked about the wonderfully clean and healthy sports and pastimes enjoyed by the Fianna in ancient Ireland – casting weights, bowling, throwing the javelin, playing endless games of hurling, hunting and a hundred other pursuits out in the fresh air that kept them healthy until they were in their nineties.

Lies, most of it! Yes, there were some activities that kept them out and about but they had many other ways of passing the time, especially during dark winter days and nights, that were objectionable, to say the least.

Examples are not difficult to find: breaking wind at each other for fun, the winner being he who could blow away his opponent, 'pick and flick', a nose-picking game, and making their water on visitors from the battlements of Tara.

But surely the most horrible one of all was *smugair-leacht* – spitting – and the surprising thing is that we know exactly where it came from and how it started.

One June in the middle of the fighting season Fionn had a most vicious dose of the flu. His throat was like a rasp, his eyes were runny and almost closed by breac; in short, he was fit for nothing but bed. And though he was a man who rarely surrendered to sickness he had to give in at last and ask permission from Cormac to go home to the Hill of Allen and take to the blankets.

'Do that!' said Cormac gruffly, 'but see Taoscán before you go.'

Why that should be necessary Fionn could not fathom but he felt too miserable to think much about it. Only when he was knocking at the door of Taoscán's cave did it occur to him that maybe the druid might have a cure to offer. But no.

'These kinds of ailments have to be allowed to take their course, Fionn. To interfere with nature is not my business. Anyway, in a couple of days you'll be fine again'.

'Easy for him to say,' sniffled Fionn as he trudged back up the hill to collect a few belongings and his dogs for the trip home. 'If he felt as I do he'd have more sympathy.'

Luckily his wife, Maighnis, was more understanding. As soon as she heard him coughing and snuffling in the distance she was out on the battlements of their home, peering, listening. She knew at once by the way he slouched along that he was not himself. Even the hounds, Bran and Sceolaing, looked dejected by his side. In the gateway he stopped and as the servants ran to meet him he waved them away.

'Keep back, if ye don't want to catch the same dose as I have.'

Maighnis would hear of no such thing, though. In her usual practical way she managed everything herself. Within minutes Fionn was stripped and put to bed, and she began to organise a meal for him – nettle soup, gruel and raw eggs.

'If they don't hunt the sickness out of him I'll think o' something worse,' she smiled as she took it to the sickroom personally.

In spite of her best efforts, though, over the next few days he seemed to get worse, not better. She began to lose her temper at last.

'You brought this on yourself! Why can't you act like a human being?' she scolded. 'In an' out o' rivers an' lakes, hunting through swamps as if you were a young lad of eighteen! When are you going to get sense?'

All he could do was look sheepish as well as miserable in the bed, for everything she was saying was true. The very evening before all this had begun he had squelched back to Tara filthy, soaked but gloriously happy, a huge wild boar held by its tail in each hand.

'They thought they'd get away from me, they did,' he laughed delighted and all who witnessed the scene smiled too. Yet Bran and Sceolaing looked anything but pleased. And Taoscán noticed it.

'Fionn,' he advised in a quiet moment, 'maybe 'tis time you stopped this kind of eejiting and let others do the dirty work. Even your own dogs look ashamed of the state you're in.'

But Fionn was in no mood for listening. Rather, he was already making plans for an expedition the following day to Móin Almhaine, where the best bog-pigs, swamp wolves and the juiciest eels lived.

But it never happened for that night his illness struck and now here he was at home in bed being treated like a baby by his wife.

It was a fate worse than death to Fionn, the bed. He hated every minute of it, especially being at the complete mercy of Maighnis and her servant women. But there was little he could do this time, for at every attempt he made to get out on to the floor shivers ran up and down through him and he broke out in a cold sweat. Time after time he was womanhandled back on to his pillows by the servants, with dire warnings of even worse gruels from Maighnis if there was any more nonsense from him. It was almost more than a warrior could bear!

But most uncomfortable of all, his throat and nose were completely blocked up and his ears buzzed constantly so that sleep was nearly impossible. Every so often he burst out into fits of cursing – half-choked and muffled, thankfully – which brought severe bouts of scolding from Maighnis. And no sword in Ireland had more edge than her tongue when she had a mind to use it.

Poor Fionn had never, ever been so frustrated in his entire life. Yet even after three days of it there seemed no end in sight. And who could blame him if, in his efforts to clear his head and throat, he was constantly coughing, bringing up huge gobs of green stuff – mucus was the name Taoscán gave it when he first visited.

'Get rid of it, Fionn, Whatever else you do, don't swallow it again or you'll be in that bed until Lá Samhna at the very least. It must come up and out if you're ever to get your health again.'

That was fine advice, and useful to have. He took it to heart, too, for at once he began – 'pthu!' – to surround the bed with huge green gobs.

'Here, stop that!' cried Taoscán. 'That's filthy,' but now that Fionn had had a little relief from what was blocking and choking him he was not about to go back to his previous state.

Taoscán glanced nervously at the door. 'Aahm ... I

think I'll be going now. Remember what I told you. No swallowing. And so, bye-bye.'

Half-way down the stairs he met Maighnis with a tray in her hands. He smiled as he struggled past her.

'Surely you're not going already? I have something nice here for you that I made myself.'

That was the problem, he knew. Again he smiled but kept backing down.

'I appreciate it, Maighnis. But there is urgent business at Tara which may not be postponed. I must be off.'

He paused at the door.

'If I were you, I'd be very careful inside the room,' and he was gone.

She shrugged, continued up, tapped on the bedroom door with her foot and . . . 'Aaaieeea!' . . . her two legs shot from under her and she landed – crack! – on the point of her bottom, then back on her poll, scattering everything on the tray.

She lay dazed for a moment while Fionn gawked at her from the bed.

'Oh-oh!' he groaned. 'Things are going to get worse.'

And he was right. As soon as she righted herself, lifted her legs and other parts, she stared a moment in disgust at what she had slipped on. At first no words came. She was too shocked for that. But when she realised that it was Fionn who had done the deed – as who else could it be? – she started in earnest:

'You . . . useless animal!' she screeched. 'You dirty savage! Out o' that bed this instant an' clean this floor, or I'll . . . I'll . . . '

He leaped out – and straight into one of the green jelly-messes. She turned away in fury.

'Yagh! Men!' was all she said more as she slammed the door, leaving Fionn feeling worse than before.

'There's no rest for the sick in this house, that's for sure,' he moaned as he tried to clean up the mess on the floor with one of the blankets.

He was scarcely back in bed when he heard heavy footsteps thumping the stairs. He coughed, shuddered and covered his head.

'What now?' he thought miserably.

It was Maighnis again and in her hand was a battered wooden bowl, one that had been used for feeding calves years before and long ago thrown into some dark corner.

'Come up out o' that,' she growled. 'I have a thing here that might improve your manners.'

He peeped out, saw the bowl and ducked back, thinking that she was about to strike him with it.

'Come out, you eejit, an' stop acting like a child.'

Again he peeped out but said nothing. He hoped she would not notice that one of the blankets was missing, for he had balled it up and stuffed it under the loose floorboard near the window.

She thrust the bowl at him.

'Any more spitting you have to do, do it into that – or you won't be able to spit!' And so saying she strode out, giving him one final baleful look as she went.

He lay watching the door for a moment but only when he heard the retreating steps on the stairs did he sit up and make the defiant gesture of launching a little spit at the door.

'Huh!' he snorted. 'Take that.' But then he thought

better of it, levered himself out, crept to the door and rubbed it off.

As he slouched back to the bed, wiping his hand on the back of his nightshirt, he looked at the bowl on the end of the bed.

'Women!' he sighed and swept it to the floor. It clattered across the boards and into the corner furthest from the bed. He rolled back under the clothes in another fit of the shivers, then dozed for a while.

He woke suddenly and sat up, shaken by a bout of coughing and spluttering. He grasped his throat and tried to get his breath, then 'Ghaa-awk!' brought up a mouthful of green stuff. He chewed on it once, rolled it twice around in his mouth and was about to decorate the floor again when a roar from Maighnis below rattled the door.

'Don't you dare! Or I'll be up with a stick.'

He stopped in amazement, his cheeks puffed out.

'How did she know?' he wondered. 'Can she even see through floors now?'

He looked around for the bowl. It was five paces away in the corner where he had driven it. He groaned and was about to get up, when he felt another cough rising. Immediately he shot the spit towards the bowl; it was either that or spatter the whole room.

Fascinated, he watched it sail across the room and 'plup!' land neatly where he had aimed it. He was so surprised that he even forgot to cough.

'That was a useful piece o' work, even if I say so myself,' and he smiled for the first time in days.

But at that very instant the door crashed in and Maighnis shouted

'I heard you spitting. Didn't I tell you to – '

She stopped, for the floor and walls were unmarked.

'Where is it?' she bellowed.

'Where's what?' he replied innocently.

'Look, don't make me mad!' she hissed. 'I want to know where that spit landed.'

'Oh, that,' Fionn smiled pleasantly, then pointed to the corner. 'There.' The bowl was half-full.

'You're not as sick as you're pretending to be if you can get out o' bed an' walk over that far to spit.'

He thought to argue, but already an exciting new idea was taking shape in his mind, one that had distinct possibilities. He must get rid of her quickly so he could think about it while it was fresh.

'Am . . . maybe that soup you gave me is having an effect. I feel a bit better, right enough. A bit o' sleep now to go with it an' I'll be on the mend in no time.'

She brightened.

'That's my grandmother's own recipe. Did I ever tell you how she got it first?'

He groaned silently. He had heard it a hundred times.

'I think you did, one time. But 'tis great stuff. Now . . . if I could only get even an hour's sleep I'd be as right as rain, I think.'

He turned towards the wall and she gave him a long last hard look before returning downstairs.

After a few extra minutes' silence, just for safety, he sat up and thought over his bright idea.

'By the heavens, wouldn't this make a great game, especially for the long days at Tara when there's nothing happening.'

He rubbed his hands in delight.

'An' if I can get enough practice before I go back I'll surely be able to impress Cormac.'

Until suppertime he cast it about in his mind and the more he thought it out the more variations of it seemed possible.

'Why didn't any of us think of it before now?' he asked himself, amazed. Over the next few days every time he heard Maighnis's voice outside he set to work spitting into the bowl, at close range first, then lengthening the distance gradually until he could fill the bowl with almost no mess on the floor around it. There were no rushed shots. Each one was considered carefully, for it was both a source of pride to him as well as a means of passing otherwise long hours.

And the dogs were happy too, for as soon as the bowl was filled to the top they were called, and for some unknown reason they were madly anxious to lap up the contents. Several times Fionn had to intervene to stop them from fighting viciously for the 'honour'.

By the time he finally left that sickroom he was smiling brightly and Maighnis could not understand such a marvellous recovery. She was suspicious.

'Was it malingering you were all the time?' she asked, when he clattered down the stairs humming and demanded his breakfast.

'Not at all. In fact, while I was in that bed I made a very important new discovery an' it could be valuable yet.'

He sat and began to eat but said no more.

'Well?' she barked impatiently, arms folded.

'Well what?' He looked puzzled.

'Are you going to tell me what was it?'

'I can't, not for a while yet. Cormac should hear it first. I think he'll be interested.'

'Huh!' she snorted. 'I'll find out anyway, whether you tell me or not.'

He knew that that was true, so it was vital to get to Tara at once and see what the reaction would be like there.

All who had seen him depart miserably for home earlier in the week were delighted to note how sprightly he now looked as he walked into the courtyard at Tara. Diarmaid was first to greet him.

'You're back to yourself, Fionn. I know by the look o' you. Was it Maighnis's gruel?' He chuckled, for her recipes were known far and wide.

But Fionn barely heard. 'Diarmaid,' he said, 'get Goll, Conán, Liagán an' a few o' the men. I have news that might concern 'em.'

Since nothing of much interest was happening that morning he was soon surrounded.

'Lads,' he said, 'I'm after making a discovery that could change the world for ever.'

There was a chorus of sniggers. They had heard such claims before.

'Are you sure you're fully recovered?' someone asked but without malice.

'I hope not,' he growled. 'Or my plan won't work.'

They eyed each other, amused. Even Diarmaid was smiling.

'You must have a supply of th' oul' heather wine under the bed, Fionn,' he joked but he quickly saw from Fionn's response that this was no joke, whatever else.

'Look, I came back here specially to tell ye something I could keep to myself if I wanted to be close about it. But I have respect for my friends. That's why ye'll listen if ye have sense. So' – and he cocked a very serious finger at them – 'shut up.'

He said it pleasantly but this was their leader speaking now. It was time to listen and they knew it. There was silence and he began to explain.

'I have a new game invented, boys. A game of skill it is, too, that'll sort out any weaklings.'

'Tell us, quick!' The word 'weakling' was of interest to every one of those fierce warriors.

They gathered in a tight huddle around him and as he explained further, heads began to nod. Anyone who had seen them from a distance would have concluded that some great story was in progress, surely. And a reasonable conclusion that would have been, because Fionn constantly invented new details as he told it, particularly about his huge struggle with Maighnis before she was at last forced to admit that it was indeed a game worthy of the Fianna of Ireland.

'She sent me here herself,' he said, 'to tell King Cormac about it personally, before someone else stole the idea. An' that's where I'm going this very minute.'

'Well, you'll be waiting a while,' said Diarmaid. 'Taoscán is inside with him. Urgent business, I'd say. So, can't you give us a bit of a demonstration while we're all here.'

Since that was how things stood, he could hardly refuse.

'All right. Goll, get a container of some type. Not too big, mind.'

Goll rushed off through the nearest door to hand, that of the feasting-hall. The servants were just then setting the tables for that night's feast when he dashed in, grabbed a wine-cup from a passing tray – 'Don't worry, I'll bring it back shortly' – and sprinted back to Fionn.

'Will this do?' he panted.

Fionn's eyes narrowed. 'Isn't that Cormac's golden wine-cup?'

'By Crom,' groaned Goll, 'you're right. I didn't even notice.'

Fionn glanced around to make sure Cormac was nowhere near.

'It'll do. This won't take long. Put it down there near the wall an' I'll show ye.'

When it was in place, Fionn stood twenty paces back, then – 'Ghllukk!' – hawked up a fine mouthful of green spit.

He closed his left eye, judged the distance carefully, then – 'Phukh!' – spat with a grace and finesse that brought sharp breaths of admiration from the watchers. Every head turned, every eye followed its flight, until it landed – 'Whlup!' – squarely into the cup.

There was a burst of cheering and applause.

'Mighty shot! Great stuff, entirely! Good man, yourself.' But when all was quiet again Conán looked at Fionn darkly, then spoke up.

'Nice one, no doubt, but maybe 'twas an accident. Could you do it again?'

'No jealousy, now, Conán,' said Diarmaid, displeased at such begrudgery. 'You saw it with your own eyes.'

'That's all right, Diarmaid. He's entitled to his opinion,'

Fionn smiled, already coughing up another green gob – 'Khaaak!'

Again he took careful aim, this time with his right eye closed, and once again – 'Pthu!' – launched the spit.

Just as before every eye was fixed on his stance, his concentration and on the flight of that missile until – 'Hluph!' – it landed once more directly in the cup.

Another burst of applause, even from Conán. There could no longer be any question of an accident. This was a game of accuracy and skill. The proof was in the cup for everyone who still might doubt.

Fionn stood back modestly. 'Now,' he said, 'if anyone here can do it better, there's his chance,' and he pointed to the cup.

Everyone was willing and soon the shouldering began for first attempt. Fionn stepped in before things could get too rough.

'No, no! Stop! This is how ye'll do it' – and he made a mark with his dagger on the ground in a half-circle round the cup. 'Now, spread out, an' each man spit when I give the word.'

They shuffled themselves into a line two paces apart, twenty paces from their target.

'Ready!' Fionn ordered, and a chorus of rasping and hacking began.

'Take aim!' They each began to size up as they had seen Fionn do.

'Shoot!' A barrage of spits was launched, and each man watched them, fascinated. But things did not go quite according to expectations. Most of the spits never even got as far as the cup and of those few that did not one hit the target.

There were surprised looks, then a hurrying forward to see what had gone wrong. Diarmaid did not have to be told. He had observed his own effort carefully and had seen the problem: his spit had dissolved into harmless spatters even before it reached half-way to the target. Most of the others' problem was the same, although Diarmaid was the one to put words on it.

'I have the range, all right, only that it broke up.'

Fionn was standing by, smiling. He spoke now.

'Didn't I tell ye 'twas a game that needed expertise an' practice, one that'd sort out the unskilled an' the weaklings.'

He walked slowly to the cup, nodding over this and that spit along the way. At the cup he turned and faced them.

'Diarmaid is right,' he said. 'I had plenty time in bed to work that out. The only way that the spit will stay together all the distance to the target is if you have a fine cold, one that blocks up your nose an' chest. An' the greener the stuff you cough up the better. If ye have any doubts look in the cup.'

They did. Carefully. Even mournfully. Then at their own efforts. It was an easy enough lesson learned. Conán voiced it, simply.

'We'll have to get a cold or the flu, that's all.'

'An' I think I know the very way to do it,' added Fionn. 'At least I have enough advice how not to.'

They looked at him. Again he was the leader, ready to advise, to guide.

''Tis like this. We have the river Boyne near us. If we stand inside in it up to our necks for a while surely to Lugh we'll get the finest flu ever.'

'How long would it take, d'you think?' asked Liagán.

Silence for a few moments.

'Different for every person, I'd say,' Fionn replied.

'Worth trying, at least,' said Diarmaid. 'When'll we start?'

'Today. No point in putting it off, if 'tis worth doing. But I'll have to talk to Cormac about it first.'

He did that shortly afterwards and made sure to keep Taoscán present also as he enthused about its possibilities for discipline, for training, for war, even for inclusion in the Tailteann Games.

Cormac was not immediately impressed.

'Fionn, I'll be honest with you. I think 'tis the most eejity idea I ever heard of. Aren't there plenty other pastimes, an' all of 'em more useful than this one you're talking about?'

Taoscán noted how Fionn's face fell and his shoulders drooped. He spoke now. 'Ahem ... Your Majesty, there's no need to be too hasty. Why not have a look at this new game for a few minutes. Maybe there *is* something in it.'

Cormac was in a benign mood that day.

'All right. We'll see it this evening when we have this problem settled of whether to invade Rome from the south or the east.'

Fionn bowed himself out to a wink and a nod from Taoscán.

In the yard he was all business.

'Right, lads! He'll see us this evening. So, everyone who wants to take part, off down to the Boyne at once an' stand in it until ye feel the flu coming.'

They had to be told only once. Word spread like the

wind of what was afoot and there was a stampede out the gate, down the hill, west to the river, followed by the curious servants. In a matter of minutes Tara was empty and silent except for a few hounds snuffling about the yard, particularly at the king's overflowing cup. In seconds they were in a struggle with each other for the honour of lapping up this delicious stuff, whatever it might be, and soon the cup was licked shining clean.

Cormac and Taoscán knew nothing of all this. Only when His Majesty shouted for a refill of wine in mid-afternoon and got no reply did he storm out ready to strike someone.

' . . . trying to run this cursed country an' no help from anyone. I'll make people pay for . . . '

He stopped.

'Where's everyone?' he roared.

The dogs looked at him, ready to run for safety. He looked around taking in the emptiness of the yard, the gates wide open. Then he saw his wine-cup lying in the dust.

'In the name o' Crom,' he breathed to Taoscán, who was now by his side, 'is the place enchanted by powerful robbers, d'you think?'

Taoscán looked mystified too but kept his head better.

'Go up there on the battlements and look around. Maybe you'll see something.'

Cormac did so, picking up his cup as he went, and sure enough off to the west he saw much activity by the river.

'Anything?' asked Taoscán.

'Come up here, quick, an' tell me if my eyes are seeing straight.'

Taoscán joined him and stared west.

'Dar fia,' he muttered absently, 'there's great excitement out there, whatever it is.'

Cormac looked again at the silent yard, then at his wine-cup.

'Should we close the gates, d'you think, an' prepare for the worst?'

Taoscán was still peering west.

'No, I don't think so. Whoever it is out there at the river, they're not coming any closer.' And after a pause he added: 'Maybe we'd better go and find out for ourselves.'

Cormac nodded. Anything was better than being in his own house in its present empty state.

It took them no more than twenty minutes to reach the river but long before that they could see that none but their own people were gathered there. And they were all staring into the Boyne.

'Maybe they're after catching salmon-poachers, an' they're drowning 'em slowly.'

Cormac brightened at the idea, because the tribes west of the river had been causing much mischief to salmon stocks of late, making it necessary for Murchadha Maor actually to buy supplies for important feasts, a situation intolerable in the High King's own house.

When at last they pushed their way through the back of the crowd lining the river bank, people began to skip out of their way and clear a path for them when they saw who was there. In a few moments they were looking down into the water. Cormac's mouth opened in disbelief at what he saw – Fionn, Diarmaid, Conán, Goll and dozens more of the Fianna sitting or standing up to their necks in the Boyne and everyone else watching them.

Taoscán also gaped for a moment but then he began to smile, taking care that Cormac did not notice. There was little fear of that. The king's voice had just come to him and he was trying to find words for what he wanted to ask.

'Fionn, are ye . . . is it so . . . am I seeing things? What in the name o' Balor are ye doing there?'

Fionn raised a hand, saluted happily. 'Trying to get the flu, Your Highness.' He turned quickly to Diarmaid. 'Any luck yet?'

'I'll see,' and that warrior, with a tremendous grating noise – 'Grnnhk!' – drew up from somewhere near his belt a mouthful of what he hoped would be green and slithery.

'Come on; spit it out for His Highness,' Fionn commanded. Diarmaid did so but, alas, it was white and frothy and soon dissolved in the water and was swept away.

'Not ready yet, Your Majesty,' Fionn shouted up, disappointed. 'But we'll stay here for as long as it takes, never fear.'

Cormac's face showed that he had no clue what all this was about. Taoscán it was who leaned close and explained:

'You remember, Your Majesty, the game Fionn described to you earlier. Well, this is part of it, I think. But let Fionn talk for himself,' and he beckoned him to them urgently.

Fionn waded out, bedraggled as a wet rat, but with fingers crossed.

'This had better be good, Fionn,' snorted the king. 'Or ye'll spend a while in the lock-up for abandoning Tara to all an' every danger an' enemy.'

Fionn waved the crowd back at least fifty paces. The others, who had clambered out of the water to watch, looked shivering at each other.

'He's being twice too confident,' whispered Diarmaid to Taoscán. 'What he did for us above at Tara wasn't half that distance.'

'This is his only chance to impress Cormac,' replied Taoscán. 'Shhh now and let him concentrate on what he's doing.'

'Get a dish,' Fionn commanded.

One was hurriedly brought and placed fifty paces from him.

'Clever lad,' noted Diarmaid silently. ''Tis three times as big as Cormac's cup was.'

A hush fell as Cormac stepped into the ring of watchers.

'Fionn,' he said, 'you have given cause for much expectation of wonderful deeds. Do not disappoint us.'

It was a command, Fionn knew, though the royal voice was hardly raised. Now was the moment of truth, when his grand new game would thrive or become a memory only.

He stepped to Cormac's side, bowed stiffly, then faced the dish. Better to make it look complicated and dignified, he thought, and dropped to his left knee, squinting now at the target. He rose then, bowed again and paced slowly the distance to the dish, circled it, head now this way, now that as he examined it carefully. As he paced back to the start line, his lips moving silently as if in calculation, he could see from the corner of his eye how impressed the watchers were, especially the king.

With a third and final bow to His Highness he turned abruptly eyes-front, gargled a moment with great effort

in his throat and nose – 'Ghaaak! Gnnkh!' – then shot out
a huge green gobshell. It arched up, up, then gracefully
down, and 'Hluph!,' landed directly in the dish.

For a few moments the air itself seemed to shiver in
silence. But then the shouting, the applause, the stamping
of feet started, expanding into a great roar of admiration
and approval. Even Cormac could not but clap, a thing
he was not accustomed to do in public.

Then Taoscán stepped forward, whispered in Fionn's
ear and beckoned the crowd into quietness again.

'There is more,' he said in his mild way. 'Observe
carefully.'

They looked at one another, puzzled, then shrugged.
What more could there be? Stranger and stranger! But they
obeyed Taoscán and watched Fionn even more attentively
while he rasped up another mouthful.

This time he seemed not even to aim or consider the
target, only spat, twice in quick succession, out of the
corner of his mouth. Again every eye followed as one,
then the other, blob of green rose and rose, then whirled
down and – 'Hluph-plup!' – landed one on top of the other
in the basin.

The applause was slower this time, because the audience was still trying to take it in, come to terms with such
accuracy. But when the yelling and hullooing started it
continued for a full twenty minutes.

Even Cormac stood, head shaking in disbelief.

When they were relatively alone within the gates of
Tara later on, Taoscán pressed Fionn's arm.

'If I didn't know better I'd say there was some draíocht
in what you did.' Then he smiled and whispered, 'You

have one convert made, anyway, to your game. Look – '
he pointed to where Cormac, accompanied by six servants
and six guards, was hurrying out and off towards the
Boyne without even a word of explanation.

In half an hour he was standing, up to his royal neck
in the river like the others, determined to take his part
in this wonderful new game of skill, spitting every so
often to check whether a ripe green flu had come on
him.

He was there only a short time, though, when the
crowd of well-wishers and encouragers on the river-bank
grew suddenly silent. Taoscán looked round quickly, and
there stood Eithne, the queen, hands on hips, glowering,
her son Cairbre and daughter Ailbhe by her side. She took
in at a glance what was happening, glared darkly first at
the druid and then raked those in the water with a grim
eye. Taoscán groaned. He knew she was bound to get the
wrong impression.

But Cormac did not seem to think so, for he called out
cheerily, 'Come on in if you like. The water is lovely an'
cold. It won't be long now before we all have the flu.'

Eithne stared at him a long while. When words came
to her they were low but very distinct in the silence. 'I
always had a suspicion I was marrying a fool and coming
to a lunatic house when I came to Tara. But I kept quiet for
the sake of the children. Now, though, they can see for
themselves what kind of an amadán they have for a father.'

The shock of the people could be felt over the silence.
This kind of talk was treason!

But Cormac kept his royal composure. He smiled,
called the children to him and with yells of glee they

bounded to the edge of the bank and leaped in, delighted for once to have permission to behave as normal children. There was a gasp of relief from the crowd and Eithne turned away disgusted and stormed back towards Tara. Taoscán noted it carefully and followed her at a distance. At the foot of the hill he called to her softly, 'Eithne! Hold back a moment.'

She jumped in fright and spun round.

'I want to be alone,' she sobbed. 'After what I saw down there at the river ... everyone laughing at my husband making a fool of himself ... '

Taoscán held up a warning finger.

'You are very wrong if you think that. Come in here to my place and I'll explain something to you.'

Faced with an empty house above she went with him and when she was seated, comfortable and holding a warm honey-smelling drink, Taoscán sat opposite her. He began quietly.

'It may seem to you that your husband is bringing your family down to the common level but that is sometimes necessary. The people must see their king in his majesty and glory in order to respect and fear him but also sometimes as like themselves, so that they may love him. What he is doing in the Boyne, I will admit it looks mad but they love it. And it has another purpose, too.'

He briefly explained to her Fionn's new game but the more she heard the more she threw her eyes towards the ceiling.

'Hasn't Cormac enough dirty habits, without teaching him more!' she exclaimed.

Taoscán smiled, for he knew them all. 'That may be,

but this one at least may have a saving grace.'

'I'll believe it when I see it,' she replied gloomily.

'Perhaps that will be sooner than you think,' he smiled.

'Look, Taoscán, I have more on my mind now than men's filthy habits. My sister is coming next week on a visit and the house was never so untidy.'

'What? I never saw it looking better. She'll like it fine the way it is.'

'Well, I don't, an' I'm going to do something about it.'

Cormac, still dripping water, was hardly in the gate when she confronted him:

'Acting the fool, when my sister will be here in a few days! Can't you put those useless gamalls of the Fianna doing something useful for once.'

'Yes, dear,' he sighed and went to get changed. She stamped her foot in frustration.

'This place, it'd drive a person to drink.'

'Talking of which,' smiled Taoscán, 'what would you say about this new game if it keeps the men here – and guests, too – from drinking too much poitín and heather wine? It'd keep me very happy and you too, I think.'

'Me? Why me?'

'Remember the treatment your furniture got from that crowd o' visitors from Bulgaria last year.'

'Very well I do. Sure most of it had to be thrown out after, even my mother's fine settle-bed.'

'And you remember what they did to your lovely goosefeather mattresses?'

'What they did *on* them, you mean!' She was almost sick at the thought of it.

'Now, all of that, for one thing, might be avoided if

Fionn's game was allowed. Under very strict rules, of course.'

'True. An' what's the other thing?'

'No more vomiting and fighting in the courtyard or behind corners by night.'

Her face brightened.

'You're a convincing man, Taoscán Mac Liath. All right. I'll watch before I say any more.'

'No one could ask better than that,' he smiled and shook her hand warmly. 'I knew I could count on your woman's good sense.'

But for how long could he depend on her hot temper?

At a meeting of Cormac, Fionn and himself an hour later Taoscán explained how he had got Eithne's temporary permission to go ahead.

'How many of the men are fit to give a demonstration now?' he asked.

'Not many,' replied Fionn sadly. ''Tis too healthy entirely they are. They came up out o' the river with not even a cough between 'em. Could you do anything, Taoscán?'

The old man nodded.

'Everything is possible, Fionn. Leave me for a little while. I must consult my books.'

When they were summoned back a short while later he held a little jar towards Cormac.

'Two drops – no more! – of this, licked from the palm of the left hand, will give you what you desire, I think.'

Cormac smiled, delighted.

'I'll be the first to try it, myself,' and he did so there and then.

'It takes at least ten minutes to work,' Taoscán pointed out, 'but well worth the wait, I promise.'

He was right, too, for while Fionn, Diarmaid and the rest, who had now been called, were carefully measuring out and applying their doses, Cormac's hands went suddenly to his throat.

'Aawgh! I feel all choked up!'

'Good,' smiled Taoscán. 'I'd be disappointed if you didn't. Now, I have to go down to the cave. I left herbs on the boil. They'll be burned if I don't see to them. But I'll be back in a few minutes. Ye're all doing fine.'

And he hurried off, rubbing his hands in delight.

It was quickly the same with all the others as with Cormac – difficulty in breathing at first, then coughing, and ringing in the ears, finally stumbling around, misery growing by the minute.

Fionn was speaking for most of them when he snuffled: 'Mby Crom, by doze id all mblocked. 'Tis a fierce ndose, mbut 'tis ngreat.'

Cormac felt much the same – 'Knaaak!' – wiping snots on his sleeves, his beautiful embroidered silk sleeves, as he sat on his golden throne.

At that moment the door was pushed in. Eithne stood there, her mouth open for whatever she had been intending to say. A look of violent disgust twisted her face and her promise to Taoscán was forgotten in the heat of the moment.

'You low savage! Is there any training the men of this cursed place, at all?'

Not a bit of notice was paid to her. There sat her husband, as contented as a pig in manure, a long green candle of snot dripping slowly from his nose, disgusting and gruesome. She stared at it an instant in horror; then hissed dangerously.

'My sister is coming shortly, an' it isn't bad enough that the house is like an animal-sty but now ye have this new filthy pastime too. I'm warning you, I'll leave you!'

'Ndon't mbind that oul' ntalk,' said he, wiping his nose with his thumb, then rubbing that to the underside of the arm of his throne.

'Stop!' she screeched. 'Are you trying to make me sick?'

'Ib sorry,' he snuffled, 'mbut I hab ad awful cold. 'tis ndeadly,' and – 'Ngaaak!' – he dredged up another mouthful, chewed it a little, then – 'Pthu!' – launched it down the hall.

At that moment Liagán skipped in the door, a bright smile on his face, when 'Splat!' – 'Awwk!' – it met him straight in the left eye.

Another man would have burst out into a litany of curses but it was Fionn who got in the first word. 'What a shot! I couldn't have done it better myself. Wouldn't you agree, Liagán.' This last question was asked in a tone of warning that Liagán could not mistake. He nodded, dumbfounded as well as disgusted.

But Cormac was anything but finished. Encouraged by his first hit he sat, clapped twice for silence.

'Watch this if ye think that one was good,' he croaked. 'Liagán, stand fast!'

'Ghaaauk!'

He squished another green one from cheek to cheek while poor Liagán trembled.

'Tphu!'

The watchers grimaced, blinked, as it spun towards its target.

'Plokk!'

It struck Liagán in the centre of his forehead, quivered an instant, then began to flow slowly down onto his nose.

The room erupted into cheers, clapping, thumping of tables.

'Great shot!'

'Mightly man, entirely!'

'The best king Ireland ever had!'

And all the time Liagán stood where he had been ordered to, the very picture of misery and degradation.

Not for long, though. A moment later he was swept aside as Cormac took a buckleap off the throne and rushed down the hall, shouting.

'Come on, men. We'll have a game this very minute. Finest thing that ever came to Tara. Who'll challenge me, hah?'

A chorus of 'yahoos' greeted this royal proclamation, and nothing Eithne could say – and she said it at the top of her voice, too – made the slightest difference. She, Liagán and Fionn were the only ones left when the hubbub and footsteps had died away and Fionn saw that he had better get a word in fast.

'Your Majesty, I'll make a small suggestion if you'll permit.'

She glared at him, jabbed a quivering finger towards him. 'You're responsible for all this. And if you don't do something about it – now! – I'll see that you're banished.'

Fionn tried to look suitably shocked but he was not too unduly worried. He had heard such threats before yet here he still was, having survived them all.

Over the next four days all usual activity ceased at Tara. Nothing now but practice, practice and more practice of this wonderful new sport. And though Eithne knew that her sister might arrive at any moment, no preparations were being made, no tidying, no painting, no food being readied. She sat almost distracted, surrounded by the sounds of spitting, unable to concentrate her mind on anything useful.

Even at night it did not cease. In the darkness of their barrack dormitory the scraping of the last dregs from throats that were already sore went on. Just as things might seem to be settling down at last a man would roll onto his elbow in the dark squishing something ugly around in his mouth. Then the cry: 'Lads, I have a grand one here. I'm working at it for the last two hours.'

Shouts then of 'Shut up!' 'Go back to sleep, you gamall!' and worse.

No good, though. He had put in too much effort to let it all go for nothing. A sulky 'Pthuph!' followed by 'Whlp!,' then a sudden shriek – 'Ahhhggh! What dirty reptile did that! I'll kill him.'

In minutes, spits flying in every direction! It was no place for the faint-hearted and that is precisely what those men were not, so on and on it went, night after night, until the room looked like a little piece of jungle, complete with dangling, dripping vines and creepers, slowly making their way – plop! plup! plop! – from the rafters to the floor.

Now all this might be excellent for training in night-fighting and accuracy in the dark but sooner or later a moment of reckoning was bound to come. And so it did.

On the morning of the fourth day, as Fionn was having his normal wash, a wet finger rubbed round each eye, one of the long green objects fell – plup! – into his wash-bowl.

'Agh! In the honour o' decency, there's a limit. No one could put up with this kind o' thing all the time.'

'You took the very words from my mouth.'

He whipped round and there stood Eithne, her eyes taking in the state of the walls, floor and roof, nausea clear in her face.

He bowed.

'Y-Your Highness! What is it that brings you here.'

For it was completely out of the ordinary for her to visit the Fianna's living quarters.

'Come outside,' she beckoned, and there in the fresh morning air she told him that her sister must soon arrive and that she needed only a small excuse to gloat.

'She always said I was a fool to marry here in Tara. Now she'll make my life miserable as she has always wanted to do – out of jealousy.'

It was obvious that only he could now see to it that all was ready in time. Or at least this was the message her manner conveyed.

'But ... but ... what is it that needs to be got ready? The place is fine, as far as I can make out.'

She sighed.

'I often wonder do men ever see anything around them. Look at the filthy state the walls are in. And that's only a start.

'If the walls are your worry, worry no more about it.' Fionn smiled, for an idea was taking shape as he listened.

'In fact, leave it to me.'

He bowed and she departed, to try to talk some similar sense to her husband, no doubt.

Half an hour later there were sixteen men of the Fianna lined up in front of the outer wall of Cormac's rooms facing the courtyard. Cormac himself was there, a little bleary-eyed but still more or less alert, observing but silent.

Fionn explained briefly what he expected:

'I want every one o' ye to decorate that wall in whatever way ye think would please Her Majesty.'

He saw them hesitate, squirm, glance at Cormac, shrug and turn towards himself, and at once he knew he had expressed himself awkwardly.

He licked his lips and was about to try again when Cormac spoke. 'Look, let there be no nonsense about this. Every one o' ye, pretend there's an enemy standing against that wall waiting to be executed. Kill him! Now!'

They saluted, faced the wall, coughed up whatever they could of spits and 'Phtu! Phtah! Phwt!' one after another did as they had been told, and not once but several times, until they could do no more. Other men replaced them then, until after four changes of personnel Fionn called a halt.

'Well, Your Majesty,' he said, not without pride. 'Will that do?'

Cormac stared at the mottled green of the wall and stroked his beard but he had no time to give an opinion, for just then the blare of trumpets was heard near at hand, then the thunder of hooves and wheels rapidly approaching.

'She's here!' shouted a guard from the ramparts. 'Princess Aoife is arrived.'

'Hell an' damnation,' groaned Cormac. 'An' we only barely started our redecorating. She always picks the worst time to come, whatever curse is on her.'

But there was nothing for it now but to appear as welcoming as possible.

Fionn had barely mustered the spitting-squad into two lines, standing to attention, when four warriors on white horses cantered in the main gate. Directly on their heels came a chariot drawn by two white stallions in which stood Aoife, the queen's sister, obviously dressed to impress.

When the formalities – peck on each cheek for Cormac, nod and smile for Fionn – were complete, she looked about her and at once her gaze fell on the newly decorated wall.

She glanced at Cormac but said nothing, only looked again and stepped towards it.

'If I didn't trust my eyes fully I'd say this was moving.'

Before anyone could reply Eithne hurried out, wearing all her finery. Aoife gave her only the briefest of salutes before turning again to the wall.

'This is the most unusual decoration I ever saw, Cormac. What craftsman did it for you?'

A look of horror appeared on Eithne's face. She recognised at once what it was.

'Sister,' she yelped, 'don't touch it!'

Her warning was too late. Aoife's fingers had made contact. And there they stopped, stuck fast to the slowly moving mass of 'paint.' She tried to jerk her hand away and in doing so clapped her other hand flat against the wall, where that, too, stuck.

Cormac covered his face with his hands and groaned 'Now I'm for it.' Fionn bit his lip and looked about nervously for Taoscán – and noticed something that made him blink, then look again. For, there was Eithne . . . smiling! As soon as their eyes met she was her serious, royal self again but the thought flashed to him that, no, there was no great love lost between these two.

He saw what must be done, though. In a few quick movements he cut with his dagger a square of the plaster and whitewash enclosing Aoife's hands and released her. Then he whispered to Diarmaid.

'Take her down, quick, to Taoscán. He'll know best what to do.'

That was done, with Eithne and several of the women-servants in attendance while everyone else in the yard kept a straight face, even Cormac.

When they were gone the hubbub of voices began and all eyes focused on the wall.

'Are you thinking what I'm thinking, Fionn?' asked Cormac.

'I'm not sure, but I think so.'

He approached the spot he had cut out. Then slowly he said.

'This could be a mighty weapon for us, not only in defending Tara but in putting all types of wrongdoers in their place.'

Cormac nodded. 'My very own thought.'

'But haven't people been spitting since the start of time,' said Diarmaid. 'How could these ones be so different now?'

'It must be the two drops of stuff Taoscán gave us, whatever he put into it.'

'I'll have to have a serious talk with him about it,' murmured Cormac. 'We don't want a thing like that getting to the wrong people.'

Then he clapped his hands.

'First things first, though. We have this evening's feast to be thinking about. Fionn, give Murchadha Maor every help he needs. We'd better try to make up to Aoife for the unfortunate ... ah ... accident that happened here or I'll never hear the end of it.'

Taoscán did an excellent job, for when Aoife entered the Great Hall that night there was no trace on her hands of anything that should not be there. Something else was obvious too: she was in the brightest of spirits, smiling left, right and centre.

'Either she's a great actor or else Taoscán worked wonders,' Diarmaid whispered as they all stood for the entry of Their Majesties.

Politeness and manners spoiled the first hour and more of the feast but after the earlier goings-on in the yard no one wished to risk giving more offence to the queen's sister. Even Taoscán's learned and witty conversation could not entirely make things seem normal.

But as midnight approached it was obvious that the guests were becoming a little more daring as the effects of drink set in. The odd belch and foolish laugh began to be heard, even wind breaking here and there wherever a guest could raise a leg without being noticed.

All this time Fionn was keeping a close eye on Aoife, wondering whether her good humour would last or whether she would even stay. In fact, he hoped she might make an early exit before drink returned the guests to full normality.

But no; she sat there smirking, watching carefully all that went on, observed in turn by Eithne, who knew very well that every vulgar incident, each lapse in etiquette, would be faithfully reported back to their father.

Sometime after the midhour of night, when it seemed that even poitín might not be enough to bring the proceedings fully to life, one of that night's three outside guests – an Ó Loineachán from the wilds of Ciarraí Luachra – heaved himself to his feet and snorted.

'Is this a feast or a funeral? Where I come from we have *real* feasts, where things happen, where our chief (the heavens rise over him!) makes sure that everyone *enjoys* himself' – he said that word in a way that left no one in any doubt that he was not doing so here and now. And he would spread the word, too. They knew that also, and did not relish the thought, for the men of Ciarraí were noted liars, famous for constructing colourful epics – the type that could dishonour even a royal house – from mere rags of fact. So it was with relief that Cormac heard Goll shout, 'What're we doing sitting here like amadáns? Throw back the tables there an' we'll show our guests something new!'

'True for you, Goll. A bit o' sense here at last!'

Fionn leaned forward. He was amazed to hear that it was Cormac who said this but His Majesty had spoken and a clearing of the floor began at once.

Cormac himself – somewhat the worse for drink now – elbowed Aoife, on his left, in the ribs.

'Watch this now, girl – hic! An' if you ever saw the like o' this for skill I'm not the Árd-Rí of Ireland.'

While she was recovering her breath from the unexpected royal elbow Cormac had staggered into the clearing in the middle of the floor, clutching his wine-cup. He grimaced, then stamped his foot.

'Quiet!' he bellowed. 'The next person that interrupts me dies!'

Silence fell like a curtain.

'There's only one person to start this, as far as I can see,' he growled, looking to every side. 'That person is me.'

He paused, looked again.

'Has anyone any better suggestion?'

No sound.

'Good. Good. Ireland isn't gone entirely stupid yet.'

He picked his way, almost too delicately, to the side of the clearing nearest the door. With care he placed his jewelled cup on the floor, straightened, swayed. Then step by step he threaded his way back to the top table, flopped onto his royal seat.

'Hit that if ye can,' he shouted.

He blinked several times before focusing on the cup.

'An' if it can be filled – an' filled right, with proper green gobs – we'll change the name o' the royal cup forever.'

He swayed in his chair, slumped, was silent. Taoscán felt it his duty to ask, 'An' what new name would be Your Highness's choice – if such a thing can be done?'

Cormac squinted, grunted, heaved several times, then rose unsteadily.

'A . . . a goblet,' he announced, surprisingly clearly.

'Goblet, eh,' smiled Fionn and the word was passed along the tables, some guests approving, others shaking their heads.

'It'll never catch on.'

'No, 'tis too strange entirely. Sure, that word was never heard in the world before.'

'Why wouldn't it catch on? Isn't it the king's own word!'

And on and on.

But Cormac was pleased with himself. That was clear from the fat smile on his face and his hands folded comfortably over his belly.

Fionn, though, was still watching Aoife. Her smirk had vanished. On her face instead was a look of puzzlement, even distaste.

'Don't tell me they're going to start ... spitting! ... into your husband's cup,' she hissed. Eithne nodded but said nothing – which reminded Fionn that someone had better get the proceedings under way. He caught Murchadha Maor's eye and beckoned urgently. It was sufficient. That experienced man of household affairs hastened to the centre of the floor, thumped his staff three times on the flagstones and in a loud voice ordered, 'Silence! The challenge will now commence. Who will be first to take his chance?'

Cormac sat up straight.

'That honour is mine,' he declared abruptly, and no one argued with that. There was utter stillness as he steadied himself, stared hard at the goblet as if it were some enemy, then placed his hands and arms flat on the table before him. All signs of drink had left him now. Slowly he began to clear his throat, in little bursts at first, then with a long rattling sound – 'Pu-haak! Kkkhh-uk!'

There was wise nodding from all over the hall. Yes, this was going to be something special, they all felt.

Two people were not impressed or approving, though,

and those two sat on either side of him: Eithne and Aoife. This time they seemed to be in agreement that what they were about to witness was mean, dirty, unkingly.

Cormac was swishing and rolling the spit in his mouth now as if he had been doing this all his life. Then he grew still, stared again at the target, inhaled through his nose, and – 'Phwt!' – spat.

But in the very instant that he did so Eithne thumped her fist into his shoulder.

'This filthiness has gone far enough!' she shouted. 'We'll be the disgrace of the whole country when word gets out.'

Cormac or the audience were not listening. All that concerned them at that moment was the royal spit.

Every eye followed it until 'Hluph!', it landed a full six inches beyond the goblet.

Silence.

Cormac turned viciously on Eithne.

'You ape!' he shouted. 'You made me miss. I'll – '

Taoscán was immediately on his feet, Fionn too, with soothing words and smiles for both Eithne and the king.

Cormac sat, smouldering, quivering with temper. But at least he said or did nothing worse.

Since His Majesty was in no fit mood to try again just now Fionn decided to go on immediately. Though he had intended not even to stand but rather to shoot in the most careless-looking attitude he could put on – elbows on table, face held between his hands as if bored – he now changed his mind. This was not an opportune moment to make the king look foolish. So, he kept both his preparations and the spit itself as low-key as possible, just a simple 'Phwt!' and 'Splup!' straight into the cup.

There was a burst of applause but it was smothered at once by Fionn for he had noticed the king's mouth tighten and he knew what that meant: envy.

Murchadha Maor was also watching closely, and he now wisely and tactfully hurried on the proceedings. Diarmaid, Liagán, Goll, Conán and anyone else who wished to try his skill was encouraged to do so. No one refused; quite the opposite. There was soon a queue, each one determined to prove himself in this game.

And a mixed performance it was, too. Some missed completely – afraid, maybe, to show up their king – some by a small margin. Only a few hit the target.

When all the accurate ones were counted Murchadha called out no more than half a dozen names (the goblet was less than one-third full yet), and so there had to be a second round.

He stood by the goblet and announced in his official voice.

'There are now six competitors left.'

He named them. Cormac was at the top of the list.

There was surprise but in spite of all the drink consumed no one showed it. This was normality. The king was first; he was the king, after all. Every one of them, no matter how stupid, knew that much. They had been reared with the idea since babyhood.

The second round produced no surprises. Fionn, of course, found the target without any difficulty, as did Goll and Oisín but the big relief was that Cormac managed to hit it too, though it seemed for several horrible seconds that his spit would topple out rather than in. To their immense relief it snailed down inside the goblet and out of sight. At least now the night's celebrations would go ahead uninterrupted.

Fionn considered the time right for a little compliment.

'Ah, Your Majesty, you have the skill. Amn't I glad I didn't put on the bet I had in my mind for that shot.'

'Bet? What bet?' asked Cormac eagerly.

'Three wild boars, no less. But 'tis all the one now. You got it in, an' that's all that matters.'

'No, it isn't,' shouted Cormac, all excited now at the prospect of winning a first public bet at this new sport.

'We'll try again. You an' me. There's no one else in it anyhow, is there?'

Goll and Oisín kept their heads down, very relieved to be out of this awkward and unwinnable equation but Fionn groaned.

'Why can't I keep my mouth shut?' he thought with a grimace.

However, there was no way out now.

Another man would simply have let the king win but that was not Fionn's way.

'Win if you can and if you must lose, do so gracefully' had always been his guiding rule, and he would not change now, even to please his king.

There was silence as Cormac prepared himself, took his stand, focused his attention. Then slowly he summoned up the royal spit –

'Gnu-nnkh!' and – 'Pfuth!' shot it towards the cup.

Silence still, mouths held open as every head turned, every eye followed it down, down until 'Hluph!' it landed perfectly in the target.

Howls of delight and pride, clapping and hammering, then Murchadha Maor's staff thumping all to silence again.

Now Fionn was the focus for each eye. And Taoscán especially looked on closely to see what choice he would make – the easy one or that which was more awkward. Fionn had made up his mind ever before Cormac's success: live or die he would give it his best.

And so he did. When his spit landed directly on Cormac's in the cup there was a pause, a darting of every eye, all attention towards the king to know how he would take it, as insult or honour.

Taoscán had no intention of allowing a witless and unproductive tit-for-tat competition to be played out that night – for he was certain Cormac would lose, with heaven knew what consequences for them all.

He rose before the absence of applause could even be noticed.

'It gives me a pleasure that is hard to put words on to witness here tonight in Tara such skill, such comradeship between His Majesty and his followers. Where else in all this land could such be found in like degree? I may safely say nowhere. But there is something even more important that should be said and it is this: a discovery has been made and its effects seen this night which may be the means of saving countless lives in the future. Let those who disapprove think as they like. We have a thing of great worth here and we know it.'

A huge round of applause greeted these words even though all their meaning might not be entirely clear. Cormac himself joined in, and Fionn.

And so the feast went on with renewed gusto. And on and on – into the following day, in fact. And so happy were all present that the food, and especially the drink, had never tasted so good. Nor did Eithne or Aoife make much objection, since there was little horseplay, cursing or rowdy behaviour. Men were too busy planning future contests, discussing the minutest details of the deed itself to allow drunkenness to get in the way.

But it would have been too much to expect that this time of unusual happenings could end with no mishap. And it did not.

Aoife, for reasons best known to herself, had taken to walking each day to the Boyne and back. Fionn, though he had no fears for her safety, offered her two guards when he found out what she was doing.

'Just to be on the safe side – an' in case you want someone to talk to.'

'Talk to? Trying to get away from people I am! I want no one even near me when I'm walking. Is that clear enough?'

He could not insist but he went to Eithne just to double-check.

'Leave her be,' she told him. 'Even when she was a girl she was like that – always off by herself. Oh I could tell you strange stories about the games she used to play by herself in the wood behind our house – as if she were talking to people in a world I could never see or know anything about.'

Fionn could sense that there was much else to this but it was more than he cared to know.

On the third day after the happy feast Aoife was

returning from her walk as usual, had climbed the hill briskly and was humming contentedly to herself as she approached the main gate. Little did she know what awaited.

Unfortunately for her that day's spitting took the form of practice in repelling would-be attackers from the gates of Tara. This had been Cormac's idea and had been agreed to by everyone as sound and useful. The target placed in the gateway was, as usual, a wine-goblet and with the most misfortunate timing the defenders stationed in various parts of the courtyard awaiting Fionn's order to fire had completed all preparations just as she approached, unseen, outside.

Inside and outside met in a split second with Aoife's stepping into the gateway, the target-zone, noticing the cup, bending to investigate and Fionn's command – 'Attack!'

As she reached for the cup – 'Someone must have dropped this' – she heard a yell.

'Stop! Get back!'

But it was too late. 'Splat! Spluk! Khlup! Whlup!' A barrage of spits and snots landed on her and around her. She staggered, fell to her knees, her beautiful sky-blue silk dress streaked and spattered, her hair beslubbered.

There was a shocked silence in the yard, utter bug-eyed consternation.

'Could we fade away, by any chance?' groaned Fionn. 'Look at the state o' the misfortunate woman.'

Only that Cormac was there, spitting as good as the next man, torture and execution might have been their lot. He took things in royal hand quickly now, rushed to her, all worry and solicitude, as if he had been an innocent passer-by.

'Oh, you poor woman! What happened?'

Then he glanced up, straightened, and stood. His face grew taut; he shook his fist towards the sky.

'Them dirty birds! They made their load on you, filthy creatures that they are, without manners or respect.'

He took her hand, raised her slowly, regally, sympathetically.

'But have no fear. I'll see to it this very day that Taoscán Mac Liath'll put a spell on 'em. He'll scatter 'em an' keep 'em well away from Tara any more.'

She did not sob or cry; she was still obviously too dazed as he led her towards the royal apartments mouthing fine-sounding words and vague promises: '... ungrateful creatures ... I fed 'em with my own hand the last time there was black frost ... but never again. They'll starve before I'll ... '

In the privacy of indoors Eithne and her servant-women at once took over. Aoife was quickly stripped of her blue (now green-blue) dress, eased into a hurriedly filled bath and scrubbed gently but thoroughly. But removing the offending snots was no simple job. Whatever Taoscán's mixture contained, sticking-power was a large part of it and much brisk handling was needed before she was clean. Her blue dress, though, was consigned to a dark corner for the time being; putting that right would be a fine punishment for a disobedient servant at another time and place. A new garment was draped over her but she herself had revived now and her shocked silence had begun to change to anger. They tried to sit her by the fire but she pushed the solicitous servants from her and when she had space enough she glared about, fire beginning to light her eyes. Her lips started to work, though there were no words for some time. It was as if she was still trying to take in what had happened her.

When she did find expression what she said was sharp, crystal-clear:

'Ever, from the first minute I came here, I knew ye were the most uncivilised crowd o' savages I ever saw. All along I did nothing about it but now I will. I'm going home this very minute to my father an' when I tell him about the dirty filths ye are an' how ye treat guests, he won't be long doing something about it!'

There was no way she could be persuaded to delay her going, short of restraining her by force, and certainly Eithne was no help at this time of crisis for she too said she was going home, that she could no longer stay in a house where such a vile practice was now an occasion of everyday enjoyment.

Aoife called for her chariot immediately and in ten minutes all was ready for departure. During that time Cormac begged, implored, tried promises and plámás, in fact did everything short of kneeling in the dust but the sisters' ears were deaf to every plea. They were leaving; that was that.

As the charioteer nervously twitched the reins, expecting every moment to be hauled down from his place by one of the Fianna, Cormac looked frantically at his wife, then at Taoscán.

'Hold a moment!' he shouted to Aoife's men. Fionn

nodded to the guards and they stepped into the centre of the gateway, weapons at the ready.

'Would ye dare even to consider offering violence to the Queen of Tara in her own house?' she spat at them.

'Violence? What violence are you talking about?' asked Cormac. 'All I want to do before ye go is get the opinion of Taoscán Mac Liath on what should be done. Are you calling him a violent man?'

Whatever else might be said no one, especially Eithne, could ever say that. He had helped her, been a friend far too often for her to offer any objection to advice from him.

He stepped between the two parties now, where all could hear him clearly and without so much as a moment's hesitation gave his advice:

'If Her Majesty wishes to take a little ... am ... holiday with her parents and sister at home, then that is what she should do.'

It was simple advice, simply given, yet it surprised all of them. He turned to go but Cormac barred his way.

'But surely ... '

'There is nothing else to say,' replied Taoscán, very formally. 'Take my advice or leave it, whichever pleases you.'

Cormac eyed him closely but the old face gave nothing away.

'All right,' he growled to Fionn. 'If they're going don't hinder 'em.'

And off they sped down the hill and away westwards leaving a cloud of dust behind. Cormac, without a word more, started for his private quarters but stopped half-way. He turned slowly, spoke angrily. 'Taoscán, a loyal servant would have made sure that they did not leave us as they have. You know well what kind of a man their father, Cathaoir Mór, is. Himself an' her foster-father, Buichead, will look for revenge on us for this so-called insult to them. Once those two men get together there'll be no talking any kind o' sense or reason to 'em. Everyone here knows that much – except you, it seems.'

He was working himself into one of his royal fits of temper. But Taoscán raised his hand now for silence.

'Cormac, do you think I acted without thought or foresight when I gave my advice just now? If so I am disappointed at your lack of trust.'

'But . . . but, they're gone home! An' that means big trouble for us.'

His voice had risen alarmingly, almost to a squawk.

'There's going to be war! D'you understand that?'

'War?' Taoscán chuckled. 'No such thing. Far from it, in fact. Last night I slept on rowan sticks I cut specially for the occasion and, believe me, the vision I saw was not of war, whatever else.'

There was no more to say, for how could any of those listening, mere king and simple warriors that they were, question the wisdom of the rowan-vision, whose truth stretched back a thousand generations?

Fionn stepped forward. 'Are we allowed to hear what your vision showed you?'

'Some of it,' replied Taoscán in his usual mild way. 'And the remainder you will witness for yourselves.'

'Explain . . . please,' smiled Cormac, feeling a bit foolish now but still curious.

'All that needs be done is send out scouts to warn of their approach. Then, when they arrive, we must seem to ignore their very presence.'

'Easy to say but not so easy to do, especially when they start to burn down this place,' said Goll sarcastically.

'Shhh!' warned Fionn. 'Let him finish.'

'I didn't say we'll be idle when they arrive,' Taoscán continued. 'No. What every person here must do is be spitting – and enjoying it so much that we seem not to even notice their existence. Of course, Fionn, be fully prepared for battle, too; that is mere prudence. But keep all weapons well hidden, though near to hand. Yet, if my vision be true they will not be needed. Not one of them.'

All this news left the listeners alternately shrugging and smiling, expecting the best and the worst all at once. But as they thought more about what Taoscán had told them they began to look forward eagerly to the coming of their noble visitors. After all, when had Taoscán ever been wrong in his predictions?

Three days later, shortly after the midday meal, two scouts who had been stationed on the east bank of the Boyne rushed into the courtyard of Tara breathless, gasping,

'They're coming! We saw 'em, thousands of 'em!'

'Right,' said Fionn briskly. 'Everyone knows what to do, so get into position, now!'

And it was true. The days since Taoscán's speech had been spent planning carefully for the arrival of their 'guests'. Taoscán, especially, had been busy, making a large supply of the spitting-compound, and there was now a quick line-up outside his cave, where every spitter was fed two spoonfuls and told to take up his position at once.

Twenty minutes later the vanguard of the coming army was seen no more than a mile off. Taoscán, Cormac and Fionn met in the yard, just inside the gates, which were wide open.

'That should shake 'em, when they see we didn't even close the gates,' chuckled Cormac but he was nervous, Fionn noted.

When they were almost within shouting distance, two horsemen galloped out from the advancing host and sped towards Tara. At the foot of the hill they paused, mystified, suspicious.

By now those within were busy at their allotted tasks and a chorus of rasping – 'Hlaaawk! Grnnk! Gnnkh! Shnrkk!' – and of spits landing – 'Pfuth! Whlopp|! Plokk!' – was all that could be heard.

The messengers looked uneasily at each other, scratched their chins but spoke no word.

Then it happened. Fionn, as had been carefully arranged, dashed out the gate, looking above and behind him, his hands waving.

'No good!' he shouted. 'You'll have to start all over again, Goll. The rules don't allow it.'

Then he stopped, stared at the silent horsemen. Acting his part exactly as he had been instructed to by Taoscán he pretended utter surprise, then horror and fright when he looked to where the huge army awaited orders to advance.

It was the messengers who spoke first, as he was waiting for them to do.

'We are here at the instructions of our masters, to demand apology and compensation from Cormac, Ard-Rí of Éireann. He has insulted Eithne and Aoife, daughters and foster-daughter of our masters.'

'An' who might those masters be?' replied Fionn, calmly now, his thumbs in his belt.

'Cathaoir Mór, Lord of Laighean, before whom the heavens tremble, and Buichead.'

'Ah, yes, I remember 'em. Fine decent men. But look, we're busy now, in the middle of practice for a terrible important challenge. Any chance they could come back later on an' we'll gladly talk to them?'

The messengers' mouths opened but their eyes could clearly see what was going on behind Fionn in the courtyard. Disbelief spread itself over their features. They were so taken aback by this and by his reply that they looked at each other, uncertain what to do.

Fionn, keeping a dead serious face, continued: 'But hold on there, now. I'll ask His Majesty if he can spare a minute.'

All they could do was nod stupidly.

Fionn strode back inside, stepped left out of sight and burst into a fit of giggling. But Taoscán quickly brought him to his senses.

'Quiet!' he commanded. 'Much depends on the next few minutes. Do as I told you – all of you' – he looked severely about – 'and no Irish blood will be spilt today.'

He faced Cormac then. 'You know what to say, Your Highness?'

Cormac nodded, gathered himself into a regal stance and strode to the gate.

The messengers dismounted at sight of him, bowed

and repeated their statement, the demands of their masters.

Cormac considered a moment, then pursed his lips.

'Tell both of them to come up here an' I'll talk to them. They can bring along whoever they like provided that there's no more than a dozen entirely. Go back an' ask if they're content with that.'

And he waved them from him.

They galloped off, and shortly afterwards a movement was noticed in the army below, a calling together of people from different parts of the ranks. When they had consulted they began to advance up the hill, led by Cathaoir, he who was most familiar with this road.

Taoscán one last time cautioned everyone to do what had been planned then walked with Cormac to the gates, smiling, welcoming.

The two parties faced each other, ten feet apart, hesitated but only for a moment. Cormac it was who stepped forward, though all of them knew it was not his place to do so. This was an honour to the visitors, an act of friendship they could not ignore if there was any breeding in them.

'My friends, it does me good to see your faces at Tara. And you are most welcome. But pardon our lack of preparation. You were not expected, and we have much in hand at present, things that will change this land forever.'

At once they were alert.

'Change? . . . Forever? What does Your Highness mean?'

'Come in an' see for yourselves.'

With sideways glances at each other they began to follow him and Taoscán, fingering their swords absently, more out of nervousness than from any fear of underhand dealing.

As they crossed the threshold and the guards sprang to attention, a strange sight met their gaze – accompanied by even stranger sounds. For there, in several different parts of the courtyard, were vessels of various sizes, each one the centre of attention of some kind: groups of the Fianna aiming, measuring, counting, commenting, hushed or applauding, clearing throats or stamping feet, all obviously fully occupied. No one paid the slightest notice to the newcomers until Taoscán clapped his hands and cried,

'A chairde, lig de, neomat! We have visitors.'

Every head turned towards the gates and there were not a few smiles of welcome as men recognised Cathaoir, the queen's father, for he had always previously been kind, generous and well-liked.

Now he and his men dismounted, clearly puzzled. But Taoscán was at work again. In a voice of command he ordered briefly, 'All right. Back to practice. Twenty more minutes left today.'

And the activity started again, diligent and intent.

'Now!' roared Lorcán, captain of the guard, 'when I give the order, everyone spit. An' let the measurers be ready!'

Under the amazed gaze of Cathaoir and his comrades a great clearing of throats and of noses began:

'Haaakk! Krrrkh! Bu-hukk! Hllukk! Mhuuunkh!'

Then followed a barrage of spits into the various bowls–

'Tphuh! Whthu! Pfu-thu! Pfuh!' – and the plops of their landing.

Not a word was uttered by the visitors, even when the measuring of hits and misses began, with all the disagreements this involved.

It was Buichead who spoke first, in a strangled voice. 'Spitting? Into bowls!'

He looked at Cormac and Taoscán as he said it, as if he were looking at strange creatures from a dark cave in the depths of An Domhan Thoir.

Cathaoir Mór was still staring, fascinated, at where an argument had broken out over some near miss. For a moment it appeared as if swords might be drawn – until – he noticed that no swords were being worn. Or daggers, either! He looked around quickly. It was the same for all the others. No one in the yard was armed except for the guards at the gates and on the walls. Odd and yet more odd!

He focused again on the argument, only to find that a referee was now closely examining the spits in question, measuring carefully. In the space of no more than thirty seconds he arose, gave his verdict. 'There's no doubt at all in my mind, Feardorcha wins this one. Sorry, Oisín. Better luck next time.'

And Oisín stepped forward and shook the hand of the obscure soldier, congratulated him and allowed the next contestant to take his turn.

Buichead was scratching his head now. He hardly noticed Fionn approach, salute him. 'A dhuine uasal, could I tempt you to take part in our humble pastime?'

Before he could accept or refuse Cathaoir stood forward, a strange look in his eye. 'I will take part,' he said.

At once he was attended by four servants, a brand-new bowl was set down for him and Taoscán himself led him by the arm to the starting-line.

'If it suits your noble self,' said Taoscán, 'no challenger

need be involved in this. Practice first a few times, for it is not as simple as it looks.'

Cathaoir brushed this aside.

'I think I may rely on my good self, Taoscán Mac Liath. I am not a child, after all.'

Please yourself,' said Taoscán with a little smile, 'but remember, none of these others are children, either, and many of them are missing their targets. If you'll take my advice you'll at least look around first.'

'I have looked enough. I know what has to be done.'

In his haste he did not hear Taoscán's softly spoken 'Ah, but 'what' and 'how' are two different things, my friend.'

All other competing in the yard gradually ceased as word spread that Cathaoir was about to perform. Men turned, then slowly, silently began to gather in close around him as he steadied himself, estimated range, then – 'Hnnkh! – filled his mouth. He chewed it thoughtfully for a few moments as he sized up the distance more carefully.

'Is Your Lordship ready?' enquired one of the four servants.

He nodded.

The servant raised his hand, then sliced it down suddenly.

'Pi-thuph!'

It was a good shot, well aimed and intended, but it never reached its destination. Before it had gone half-way it dissolved into the same spatters as the early Fianna efforts, and Taoscán smiled a little smile and nodded gently as he saw the surprise on Cathaoir's face.

'Are you certain, Your Lordship, that you wouldn't have a bit of short practice first?'

Cathaoir snorted and tried again – with the same result. Those standing about nearby, even Buichead, turned away, not wishing to embarrass him, but it was easy to see that most were secretly pleased. Now, perhaps, he would start at the beginning, as they had had to do.

This time, when Taoscán offered his advice he was listened to. He led both visitors out of the yard, down to his cave and there dosed them with his magic potion.

'Get ready to feel unwell,' he cautioned when they had each swallowed the two spoonfuls, 'but don't be worried. In ten minutes' time the world will be a different place.'

He left them wondering what this kind of talk could mean and went off about some business he had in hand. But always he was eyeing them, watching for panic or terror as the symptoms of flu grew on them. And grow they did – headache, coughing, feeling miserable, blocked throat and nose, then finally buzzing ears.

Cathaoir began to gasp, cleared his throat – 'Bhh-kk' – and was about to spit on the floor when Taoscán cautioned sharply.

'No! Don't do that!'

Cathaoir turned angrily. He was unused to being told what not to do. But Taoscán held up a finger of warning.

'Think a moment! Can you do nothing better with that spit than fling it on my floor?'

Silence.

Buichead might have said something but just then he was beginning to cough and show all the same symptoms.

Cathaoir chewed over Taoscán's question, but suddenly stopped when he realised that it was something else entirely he was chewing. His fingers went to his lips and he pulled forth a long streamer of greenery, almost an arm's length of it. Before he could say a word Taoscán advised, 'Go back now to the yard above. See how much you have improved.'

It was the advice of a lifetime, for a few minutes after his two visitors, despite all their flu symptoms, had rushed off up the hill Taoscán heard a wild yell from the courtyard:

'Ya-hee! I got it in. First time, too. Keep back till I try again.'

'No! My turn now!'

From that time on Cathaoir and Buichead were among the new sport's greatest enthusiasts, and both went on to do great things in the years that followed. Cathaoir even managed to convince Eithne and Aoife to forget their differences with Cormac and give it a try, and though they both obeyed their father's wishes it was never with much enthusiasm that they did so, even when Cormac made a large sack of gold available if they – Eithne especially – would organise a women's spitting league.

Still, as long as they put no serious obstacles in the way of the men's competitions there was general contentment.

And what competitions there were! – all manner of leagues, combinations, associations and incorporations sprang up in every part of Cormac's dominions and it was hoped by all civilised people that it would mean the end of fighting and sword-play between the tribes of Ireland. But that was a forlorn hope. For in all this enthusiasm for the new pastime there was naturally much confusion, every team wishing to play to its own strengths and hide its weaknesses. Within a short time Fionn's noble new sport, much to his disgust, was being used as a pretext for violence rather than a cure for it. 'Hi, crooked-eyes, you spat on my sandals. Lick it off, or, by Lugh, I'll wipe your face in it!'

'Gobdaw, you're like your father. If your hooves weren't so big . . . '

And on it went.

At last, after spending a whole hunting season trying to settle squabbles like this up and down the country – a most thankless job – Fionn staggered, exhausted, to Taoscán.

'We'll have to have rules,' he said. 'That's all there is to it.'

'I couldn't agree more,' replied Taoscán. 'But who's the one to do it?'

'That's why I'm here. Didn't you tell me a while ago that there's a druids' meeting coming up soon. If you talked nice to a few of 'em maybe . . . '

Taoscán laughed.

'Always the same. Come to me when ye can't solve even the simplest thing.' But he was not annoyed, Fionn could see, but rather pleased to be asked.

'All right,' he said. 'I'll see what I can do.'

And he did. When the druids' meeting of that year at Cashel was in session he brought up the problem during some light conversation – and found an immediate audience. For several of the druids had already seen the competitions in practice and some had even provided a concoction like his own to improve the quality of spits.

It was decided to let some of the younger druids work on the matter if they wished. And wish they did! For this was far more exciting than attending to deep lectures by ancient experts on complex learned matters that they knew little of. Within three days, working furiously, while some of their friends took notes on the serious sessions for them, they produced a document which surprised Taoscán, Mogh Ruith, Lochrú, Fíodh Mac Neimhe and other old masters by its thoroughness.

Kinds of spits were dealt with: seile, seileog, seilín, gobseile, crainn-tseile; then there were smuga, smugaid, smugairle, smugairlín, smugail, smug-sheile. Each one was clearly defined as to its type, colour, weight and consistency. The height of spitting was limited, as was distance, for each and every type of competition. Age-groups were set and certain exclusions were made. For example, the sons and daughters of druids were prohibited from taking part – not because it was felt that any such father would betray his trust by illegally helping his child or hindering other competitors but because it might distract such a one from his more serious and pressing duties to his lord or king.

The older druids smiled when they read this but decided to let it stand as a reminder of humility to all of them.

Duration of contests was fixed, as were the days on which none could be held – Lá Bealtaine, for example.

Additions had to be made, of course, and other items dropped, but overall it was a document that pleased the elders greatly, and Taoscán summed up the feelings of practically all when he said,

'There's hope for Ireland yet when the youth of the country can produce the like of this.'

It was the basis, with few other changes, for almost a thousand years of this wonderful game in Ireland – from where it spread to a large part of Europe. There it replaced such disgusting pastimes as Bavarian vomiting contests, Bulgarian head-banging, Spanish hair-tearing, German ear-biting and Carpathian gut-twisting. Only in the evil reign of that man of notoriously poor judgement, Henry VIII (under Act 881/2 of the Dublin parliament, a servile and corrupt body if ever there was one) was it finally outlawed in Ireland after much prompting by a drunken archbishop of Dublin who had been spat at by his congregation four Sundays in a row on account of his idiotic sermons and presented with bowls of snots for his Yuletide offering, as part of an elaborate Irish joke.

Yet it did not finally die out until the latter years of the reign of George IV, when Daniel O'Connell, trying to make the Irish respectable enough to vote, proclaimed that: 'Spitting is a filthy habit brought here by the English to bring us down to their own level.'

That finished it as an organised sport. A pity, and a sad end to a noble custom, one that gave great joy to the people of Ireland in good times and in bad alike for over a millennium.

[1]For the case of Galar (pp. 81-2) see *Gruesome Irish Tales for Children*, Mercier Press, 1997.

GLOSSARY OF IRISH WORDS

A dhuine uasal	Formal, rather impersonal greeting – *lit.* 'noble person'
Amadán	A fool
An Domhan Thoir	The Eastern World
Aoibheall	Otherworldly protectress of the Dál gCais sept
Ard-Rí	The High King of Ireland
Ball seirce	A love-or beauty-spot.
Balor	Fearsome mythical figure whose poisonous evil eye could destroy whole armies
Bothán	A small, miserable house
Breitheamh	A judge
Breac	Sleep-crust in the corners of the eyes
Brú na Bóinne	'The Palace of the Boyne', a group of stone-age burial-places in the Boyne valley near Slane, County Meath
Cailleach	A hag
Cam	Crooked
Carraig Aoibheall	A limestone outcrop on Craglea Hill in east Clare where Aoibheall appeared at times of great significance for the Dál gCais
Ciarraí Luachra	A sept that inhabited the area around Tralee Bay in Kerry
Cluaisín	Little ear
Crannóg	A lake-dwelling
Cúl Bán	Present-day Coolbaun, on the eastern side of Lough Derg

Dál gCais	A sept of east County Clare
Dar fia	By the Lord (mild imprecation)
Dearg	Red
Draíocht	Magic, enchantment
Dún	A fortified dwelling
Fiaclóir	A dentist
Fulacht fiadha	Ancient cooking-place
Gamall	A person of low intelligence
Garbhán	A coarse, boorish person
Gath Dearg	The Red Spear
Gleann na nGealt	The Glen of the Madmen, modern-day Glenagalt in the Dingle Peninsula in County Kerry
Lá Bealtaine	The first day of May
Laighean	Leinster
Lár na hÉireann	The centre of Ireland
Lá Samhna	The first day of November
Leithreas	A lavatory
Liúdramán	An awkward, foolish person
Lúbán Díge	Present-day Bodyke in County Clare
Lug	An ignorant fool
Lugh	Celtic god, possessor of all the arts
Maor	A steward
Móin Almhaine	The Bog of Allen, in County Offaly
Muscraí	Present-day Muskerry in County Cork
Oileán Mór	Present-day Illaunmore in Lough Derg, *lit.* 'Large Island'
Ómós	Honour, respect
Ortha na seacht lúb	The charm of the seven twists
Pililiúing	Whinging, crying
Plámás	Flattery, soft talk
Poitín	Home-distilled liquor

Ráiméis	Nonsense
Reacaire	Reciter of poems
Seile	A spit
Seileog	A spit
Sliabh Luachra	An area on the Kerry-Cork border, north-east of Killarney
Smuga	Snot, thick spit
Smugairle	Thick spit
Tailteann	Present-day Teltown in County Meath, site of ancient annual assembly and games
Tráithnín	A little blade of grass; something insignificant
Tuatha Dé Danann	A divine otherwordly race, *lit.* 'The People of the Goddess Danu'
Uisce Beatha	Whiskey, *lit.* 'the water of life'

Stad den tactadh, cara mo chroí;
lig beo é fós do chúirt an dlí.
Stop choking him, friend of my heart;
let him live yet for the court of law.

A chairde, lig de, neomat
My friends, pause a moment